GUNS AT GRAY BUTTE

Also published in Large Print
from G.K. Hall by Lewis B. Patten:

Gun Proud
Villa's Rifles
The Angry Town of Pawnee Bluffs
Cheyenne Captives
Hunt the Man Down
The Killings at Coyote Springs
Red Runs the River
The Trial of Judas Wiley
The Law in Cottonwood

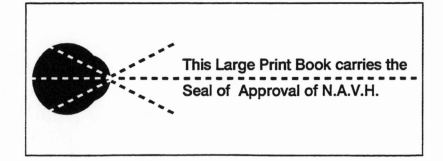

GUNS AT GRAY BUTTE

Lewis B. Patten

G.K. Hall & Co.
Thorndike, Maine

Published in 1995 by arrangement with the Golden West
Literary Agency.

This novel is a work of fiction. Names, characters, places, and
incidents either are the product of the author's imagination or
are used fictitiously, and any resemblance to actual persons,
living or dead, events, or locales is entirely coincidental.

G.K. Hall Large Print Western Collection.

The text of this Large Print edition is unabridged.
Other aspects of the book may vary from the original edition.

Set in 16 pt. News Plantin.

Printed in the United States on permanent paper.

Library of Congress Cataloging in Publication Data

Patten, Lewis B.
    Guns at Gray Butte / Lewis B. Patten.
        p.   cm.
    ISBN 0-7838-1157-8 (lg. print : hc)
    1. Large type books. I. Title.
[PS3566.A79G86   1995]
813'.54—dc20   94-33679

GUNS AT
GRAY BUTTE

Chapter 1

NO

Gray Butte was a sentinel, brooding and tall on the western edge of town. It began to rise in the center of town and, less than two hundred yards from the last building, pitched up in perpendicular grandeur to its crest five hundred feet above.

Now, the rising moon put a silver shine on the sheer rock face. In winter huge pieces had sometimes broken away to roll crashing through the town built with human impracticality at its foot.

At ten, most of the town slept. There were lights in the Butte Saloon, in the Buffalo Saloon, in Delehanty's Mercantile Store and in the sheriff's office at the lower end of Butte Street, which was Gray Butte's main thoroughfare.

A solitary figure walked the street, Julie Duquesne, heading up Butte toward the Duquesne house nestling in the shadow of the sheer rock face.

She walked with a free, swinging step that was almost a skip, and a couple of times stopped to turn her head and look dreamily at the rising moon.

She carried a small package of ribbon and was coming from a fitting at Cora Short's dress-making shop, the last fitting before her wedding gown would be done.

Julie Duquesne. A slight, small girl almost boyishly slim. A girl with wiry strength, with the delightful litheness of the very young. A girl with a half-smile on her lips, with brightness and a sparkle in her eyes. A girl who would be married a week from Sunday next and who could scarcely wait.

She heard movement beside the abandoned Satterlee house and turned her head without fright. She saw the figure there, a man's figure, detaching itself from the shadow of the porch to come toward her at an unsteady, hurrying walk.

Startled, still no fright stirred in her. She stopped, and stared, trying without success to recognize the man. She did not think to run. Gray Butte was a town in which no woman need fear to walk the streets at night.

Too late she realized the man did not belong in Gray Butte. He was a stranger and a drunken one. She turned to run as he reached the sagging gate, but he slammed it back, lunged through and seized her before she could take more than a couple of steps.

She opened her mouth to scream, felt a dirty hand clamp itself over her nose and mouth, suffocating in its brutal strength. She felt herself lifted and carried back through the gate toward the dark and abandoned house.

She kicked with sudden terror and tried to bite the hand that was suffocating her, without success. It was clamped too tight. She struggled with every bit of her strength but it did no good. She was held in a vise, by strength many times greater than her own.

Hysteria seized her, frantic hysteria that gave her added strength. Yet still those iron arms and hands held her and the man didn't seem to notice her kicking feet or clawing hands.

His breath came in short, fast gusts, strong and nauseous in her face. He kicked open the door of the vacant house and carried her inside.

Holding her against him with the hand clamped over her mouth, he literally tore the clothes from her body with the other. Then threw her to the floor.

Too terrified, too hurt to scream, she could only moan now, "Please. Oh my God, please . . . !"

But it did no good. There began for her the most terrifying, the most horrible experience of her life. Now, her struggles angered him. Animal grunts came from his lips and his fists smashed into her face, driving away what little consciousness was left until she lay limp and unconscious and unresisting.

Pain came first with returning consciousness, and ugly horror, and overpowering shame. The house was quiet as a tomb. She was all alone.

Bleeding and naked and stunned, she tried to rise and failed. She crawled along the floor, groping for her clothes. Finding only shreds and rags, she pulled herself erect by using a straight-backed chair that had not been overturned.

Trembling, stunned and unable to think, she staggered toward a door, stumbled through it and fell upon a bed. The coverlet smelled of dust, but she wrapped it around herself and for several minutes lay there shivering and sobbing uncontrollably.

One thought towered enormously in her shocked mind: an hour ago her life had been a bright, clean, happy thing. Now it was ruined and done.

Slowly her trembling quieted. Slowly her mind began to function again. Anger entered her thoughts. And hate for the animalistic beast who had done this thing to her.

Nothing could restore that which had been taken away. But the man could be made to suffer too.

She got to her feet, the dusty coverlet still wrapped around her body. She stumbled from the room to the open outside door.

She staggered into the yard, down the walk and into the street. Now, even the lights in the two saloons were gone. Gone too was the light in Delehanty's Mercantile. But there was still a light in the sheriff's office and jail.

For only an instant did she hesitate between her home and the sheriff's office. Then she fled down the hill toward the beckoning light. It was all she could do to keep from screaming hysterically into the dark and silent night.

Pete Chaney sat in the sheriff's scarred swivel

chair, his booted feet on the desk. There was in unaccustomed nervousness in him tonight that he did not understand.

It was probably the thought of getting married in little more than a week, he decided with a rueful grin. Marrying Julie Duquesne was enough to make any man nervous. Nervous for fear something would happen before the date set for the wedding.

A big, rangy, loose-muscled man was Pete, twenty-five on his last birthday. He'd been deputy sheriff of Butte County since Jess Stone took office a little less than two years before.

His eyes were ice-blue, his hair the color of weathered straw and cut fairly short. His mouth was wide and usually easily smiling. But it could turn hard and the combination of hardness in ice-blue eyes and mouth took all the easygoing quality from his face.

He tossed his wheat-straw cigarette into the spittoon, hauled his feet off the desk and got up. The chair creaked thunderously.

Pete paced to the window, then back to the barred door leading to the cells in the rear. He kicked the bars. Maybe he ought to go home and go to bed. He didn't have to stay. There was no one in jail tonight.

He walked to the window and stared outside again. The street was dark — too dark to see anything but the vague outline of store buildings across the street. The odd uneasiness he had felt before increased.

Something caught his eye upstreet toward the butte and he stared more closely. He yanked open the door and stepped outside. He heard her hysterical cries only briefly. Then she reached him and he caught her in his arms.

She tried to talk and failed. He picked her up in his arms, carried her inside and kicked the door shut behind him. He said, "Julie!" in a shocked, unbelieving voice. "What happened? For God's sake, what happened!"

"A man." She was shaking uncontrollably. Her teeth chattered audibly.

"Who?" A terrible stillness was in Pete Chaney's voice. A fury was in his eyes, fury that made them burn.

Her head was buried against his chest. Her trembling did not subside. "I don't know. He was hiding in the yard beside the Satterlee house. Oh God . . . !"

His arms tightened around her as though their strength could stop her trembling, drive away her terror. He said softly, "I'll get him, Julie. I'll get him."

He felt helpless, holding her. Helpless to give her the comfort she needed. He stared down at her tear-streaked face. Her lips were cut, bleeding and beginning to swell. One of her eyes was bruised and turning black. There was a raw, bleeding abrasion on one of her fine cheekbones.

"Do you want me to take you home?"

"Not yet. Please Pete, not yet."

He carried her to the office couch and put her

down. He knelt beside her helplessly. She needed him; she could not be left alone. But while he waited here, the attacker was getting away.

He got up, dumped cold water into the pan on the washstand and soaked a towel in it. He wrung it out, took it to her and gently dabbed at her bleeding face.

Julie's stricken eyes met his painfully, shamefully, and her lips made the almost silent words, "Kill him, Pete. Catch him and kill him. Make him pay, because we can't be married now."

"The hell we can't! Don't you talk that way. You've been hurt, but that's all that's happened to you. You'll heal. This isn't going to change a thing."

The look in her eyes right then made him want to kill the man — with his hands. She said in a scarcely audible voice, "Nobody wants a girl that . . ." She couldn't go on. Her sobs and her trembling increased.

Pete said, "I'm going to take you home. Then I'm going to get the doc for you."

She did not protest. Her expression was filled with despair, with hopelessness. He picked her up and looked down into her face. "Julie, I'm not lying. I'm not being noble, either. I'm being just plain selfish. I'm not going to let you go."

He wasn't sure she heard or if she did whether she understood. A strangely vacant look was coming into her eyes, a look that frightened him. He went out, carrying her, and strode up Butte Street toward her home.

13

He reached it quickly, kicked open the gate and went on up the walk. He kicked on the door and waited impatiently. Julie's trembling had stopped and he couldn't see her face. But he had a feeling that something even more awful had happened to her during the short walk up the hill. He remembered the strangely vacant look that had begun to come into her eyes before he started here with her.

Through the stained door glass he saw a lamp coming toward him. The door opened.

He said harshly, "It's Pete. I've got Julie here and she's been hurt."

He carried her inside. At first there was stunned bewilderment from Julie's father. Then there were questions, all but shouted at Pete. Then there were hysterics from Julie's wrapper-clad mother.

He tramped upstairs to Julie's bedroom and laid her on the bed. He stood looking down at her, at the numb expression on her face, at the terrible, withdrawn expression in her eyes. Physically she would heal. But the shock . . . its effect on her mind . . .

His face twisted. He looked at Julie's father, at her hysterical mother. He said, "For God's sake, pull yourselves together. Julie's been hurt, you haven't. Give her something besides hysterics. She needs help. She needs you now more than she's ever needed you in her life."

His voice — its harshness — the words he used — he didn't know which had the most effect. But he seemed to have gotten through to them. He said, "I'll go get Doc."

He ran down the stairs and out into the night. He ran all the way to Doc's house two blocks away. Puffing, he hammered on Doc's door upon which a sign hung, "Rufus Bonner, M.D."

A lamp flickered somewhere in the depths of the house. The light grew as it approached the door. Doc appeared and opened it, carrying the lamp, clad in a long white flannel nightshirt, his thinning gray hair tousled.

Pete said, "Get dressed, Doc. Julie's been hurt!"

"Come in." Doc's voice was hoarse but wide-awake.

Pete went in and closed the door. Doc peered at his face a moment. He turned away and headed for the bedroom, but his voice came floating back. "Hurt? How?"

"A man. A stranger she said. He caught her as she was going home from Cora Short's."

"Did he . . . ?"

Pete's body felt cold at Doc's avoidance of the word. He said in a tight, angry voice, "Yes, and beat her. There's a look in her eyes . . . it scares hell out of me, Doc."

Doc came through the door. He had pants and shoes on now and was putting a shirt on over the upper half of his nightshirt. The lower half made a bulge where it had been stuffed untidily into his pants.

He finished buttoning the shirt and stuffed it similarly into his pants. He grabbed his coat and hat, picked up his scuffed bag from the table beside the door. "Come on."

He went out and Pete followed, closing the door behind. "You get the man?"

"No, but I will." He matched Doc's hurrying pace. The worry kept growing in his mind. "Will she be all right, Doc? Does a woman get over a thing like this?"

"Some do. Goin' to call off the wedding, are you?"

"Are you crazy? This isn't Julie's fault."

Doc grunted. He asked skeptically, "How about later? How about when the whole town knows?"

"They won't . . ." He stopped, because he knew that wasn't true. What had happened would get out no matter how he and Julie's parents and Doc tried to keep it from getting out. He growled, "What difference will it make . . ."

"Maybe that depends on you." They reached the Duquesne house and went up the walk. Julie's father was waiting in the doorway.

Doc went upstairs. Pete could hear Julie's mother crying up there somewhere. He looked at Jules Duquesne helplessly. The man said, "Get the bastard, Pete. If it's the last thing you ever do."

Chapter 2

Pete went out and closed the door. He stood for an instant on the porch, scowling. He looked down at the town and saw that it was no longer dark.

Half a dozen houses between here and the center of town were blazing with light. He hurried down the street toward the vacant Satterlee house carrying the lantern he had borrowed from Jules Duquesne.

Del Pomeroy was waiting beside his gate several houses downstreet from the Duquesne place. He said, "Pete . . . was that Julie you carried up here? You need some help?"

Pete felt helpless and trapped. Pomeroy had obviously been busy in the last half hour. He must have seen Pete carry Julie up the hill and he hadn't wasted any time if the number of lighted houses was any proof. He said sourly, "All right, Del. Come on."

"What happened?"

"A stranger. Julie . . ." He stopped, not wanting to go on.

"The dirty bastard!" There was quiet, murderous outrage in Pomeroy's voice.

In Pete, the shock was beginning to wear away. In its place was raging fury greater than anything he had ever felt before. And hate so powerful it was like a sickness in his mind. He wanted his hands on the man. He wanted to tear him apart.

By the time he reached the Satterlee house, there were five men following him. Some carried shotguns, some rifles. Their talk was hushed but angry. He stopped them at the gate. "Wait here. I'll see what I can find."

He went up the walk and into the open door of the house. He saw the ripped remnants of Julie's clothing. His eyes, in the lantern light, took on a savage, burning glow that was all their own.

He put the lantern on the table, then went around picking up the scraps of Julie's clothing. When he had gathered them all, he took an embroidered scarf from a table and wrapped them in it.

Now he searched more minutely, the fury in him smoldering. He wanted a trail to follow; he wanted to be riding. But there would be no trails until daylight came; there would be no pursuit until then.

Though he searched the entire room, he found nothing. Except for some drops of blood that were probably Julie's.

Carrying the lantern and the scarf-wrapped clothing, he went outside again. He said, "Del, go wake the sheriff."

Del Pomeroy hurried away. Pete said, "One of you go wake Lex Massey and find out if any strangers were in the saloon tonight. Somebody else go talk to Frank Hight. If they remember anyone, get a description of them."

Two more of the men moved away. Pete said, "The rest of you go home and go to bed. We can't do a thing as long as it's dark."

He watched them go, obviously reluctant. He scowled fiercely, thinking of Julie, beaten, bleeding. He remembered her terror, her voice, her stricken eyes that had, at the last, been so withdrawn.

He cursed softly, bitterly, under his breath. Hatred made a nauseous sickness in the pit of his stomach. He could kill tonight, deliberately, coldbloodedly, gladly. Tonight only that could erase the memories crowding his mind.

He started down the street toward the sheriff's office. His hand went up unconsciously and fingered the star on his vest.

Feeling as he did, he had no right to wear this star at all. Because if he wore it he would dishonor it tomorrow.

But his hand came away, leaving the star still pinned to his vest. The law was a career in the Chaney family. His grandfather had served with the Texas Rangers until his death. His father had been sheriff of Butte County for more than twenty years.

Abruptly he turned, taking a side street leading

right off Butte. He strode swiftly now, purpose-
fully.

At the end of the street where it petered out
in a two-track road leading to the dump, he turned
in at a weed-grown, small frame shack. He
pounded on the door.

After a while a lamp went on. An irritable, deep
voice called, "Come in. Come on in, damn it!"

He went in. His father put the lamp on a table,
ran a hand through his tousled mane of graying
hair and reached for his pants. He put them on,
then sat down in a chair next to the light.

He was a gaunt old man, a bit taller than Pete's
even six feet. His frame had plainly been built
to carry twice the weight it now carried. There
were scars on his face and on his hands. There
were other scars too that didn't show, thought
Pete, on both his body and his mind.

But his eyes still possessed some of their old
sharpness as he glared at his son. "It better be
important," he said, "waking me up in the middle
of the night."

"It's important."

"What is it, damn it? What is it?"

"Julie. Some stranger mauled her on her way
home tonight."

"Raped her you mean?"

"That's what I mean, damn you. Beat her with
his fists too."

"So why are you coming to me? Go get him.
Or do you need me to tell you how to do your
job?"

Pete said, "I know my job. That's why I'm here."

"What the hell are you talking about?"

"I can't trail until it's light. I've got until then to make up my mind. If I go as sheriff's deputy I'm sworn to bring him back. I'm not sure I can bring him back or even that I want to. Right now all I want is his dirty neck between my hands."

The certainty, the sureness, suddenly went out of Jacob Chaney. Unwelcome memories aged him ten years in a few minutes. The sharpness left his eyes to be replaced by confusion. He stared emptily at the floor between his feet.

Pete had his answer, the one he had come here to get. His father had once been strong and sure and tough. Fast with the gun he carried at his side, carrying the scars of a dozen gunfights with a dozen men who should have been faster than he. He had been the law in Butte County when there was no other law.

In those days when judges rarely came through on circuit, when juries could be intimidated or bought, too often he had taken it upon himself to serve as judge, jury, executioner. Too many of Jake Chaney's prisoners had been killed resisting arrest and brought in dead.

Drastic methods for drastic times, they had brought orderliness and law to a county that had never known it before. But power made Jake Chaney arrogant. Some people said it made him feel like God.

Jake looked up slowly. He said, "If you wear

that star, you bring him back. If you figure you've got to kill him, go without the badge." He wrung the words from some deep recess of him without looking up at Pete. He spoke them as though by rote, in a dead and lifeless voice.

Pete turned away and the lifeless words followed him. "Before you kill, be sure it's him. Then play God if that's what you have to do."

Pete said, "Thanks, Jake. Sorry I woke you up."

"It's all right. I don't sleep too damn well anyhow. Good luck."

Pete went out into the dark, still night. He stood in the cluttered, weed-grown yard a moment, scowling. He remembered the last man Jake had killed. He'd been fifteen and had watched Jake come into town, riding a dusty, sweaty, beaten horse and leading another just like it. He'd seen the dead man Jake brought in, a youngster that wasn't twenty yet. He'd seen the eyes, dull and bulging because the head hung down. He'd seen the tongue, black and swollen and lolling out. . . .

He'd been proud of his father that day. Proud, even if he was a little sick at his stomach. Then a week later, a bunch of townsmen caught another man robbing a store. And scared him enough to make him confess the killing of which the dead young man had been accused.

Pete remembered something else he had long tried very hard to forget. His father's muttered, half-incoherent talk as he lay tossing in his bed at night. The way Jake Chaney changed in the next six months from an overpoweringly strong and virile man into what he was right now.

Angrily he strode up the street. He turned on Butte with a long stare at the now-dark Duquesne house and headed down the hill toward the jail and sheriff's office, which was ablaze with light.

Hell, maybe he was making a mountain out of a molehill. Maybe he'd never have to make the decision at all. Perhaps the fugitive wouldn't give himself up. Perhaps he'd fight and Pete would have no choice but to bring him in dead.

He thought of Julie and felt his fury grow again. He was a fool to worry about killing an animal like that. Besides, what difference did it make? Even if he brought the man in alive he'd never go to trial. The town would lynch him, string him up from one of the cottonwoods at the lower end of town.

He reached the stone-block jail and went inside. Jess Stone, the sheriff, was there. So was Lex Massey, Frank Hight, Del Pomeroy and the two Pete had sent after Massey and Hight.

Stone was a short and stocky man with a heavy stubble of graying whiskers on his weathered cheeks. He had reddish hair that was receding over his high forehead and thick, stubby hands with thick, stubby fingers on the backs of which a heavy growth of red hair grew. Not a gunman. Not a fast man with a gun at all. A methodical, stubborn, slow-moving man who never went after a fugitive without a posse at his back. But a man who never came back empty-handed either.

Stone looked at Pete, his eyes hard but holding a certain sympathy in their depths. "What happened, Pete? Tell me everything you know."

Pete said, "I was here, thinking about going home to bed. I stepped out front a minute and there was Julie, beaten and hysterical and wrapped in a blanket she'd snatched up off a bed. She said she was going home from Cora Short's when this man jumped out from beside the Satterlee house. He grabbed her and dragged her in."

He laid the bundle of clothing on the desk. "I went back after I got her home and gathered these."

Stone stepped toward the desk. Pete said, "No. Leave 'em be. At least until we're alone."

Stone stopped without touching the bundle. Pete said, "I'd have kept it quiet if I could, for Julie's sake. But Del Pomeroy happened to see me carrying her up the hill. Time I got out he had half the neighborhood awake."

Stone glanced at Pomeroy. "What do you do, sit by that window of yours all the goddam time?"

Pomeroy flushed. "You ain't being fair, sheriff. It's just that I don't sleep too good. When I can't sleep I sit by that window and look outside. Anything wrong with that?"

Pete glanced at Massey and then at Hight. "Any strangers around tonight?"

Massey shook his head, but Hight nodded. "A couple. Both of 'em drifters, looked like."

"They together?"

Hight shook his head. "No. Didn't seem to

24

know each other at all."

Something cold began to grow in Pete. He had hoped it was going to be cut and dried. But with two strangers in town tonight it wasn't going to be. He didn't see how he was going to get a decent description of the man out of Julie. It had been dark and except for size she wouldn't be able to tell him much even if she was coherent enough to talk about it. And he doubted if she would be for a long, long while.

He asked harshly, "What'd they look like?"

Hight frowned. "I'll try to remember. Jesus, Pete, there's strangers passin' through all the time. Man gets so he doesn't even notice them."

"Try."

"All right." The frown on Hight's face deepened. "Seems like both were good-sized men. Your size maybe. Cowhand clothes on 'em both. Dusty. Dirty. One was ragged and didn't wear a gun. The other did." His frown deepened. "That's about all I can tell you, Pete. I'm sorry."

"Think on it. Maybe you'll think of something else."

"All right, Pete. If I do, I'll let you know. Is it all right for me to go home now? I'm kind of beat. It was too damn hot to sleep tonight."

Both Stone and Pete nodded in unison. Stone said, "The rest of you go home too. We'll send for you if we need you."

"You're gettin' up a posse, ain't you?"

"Likely. I'll let you know."

They filed out. Stone looked at Pete. "You

thinking what I am?"

Pete said, "The hotel. And the livery barn."

"Let's go." Stone blew out the lamps and followed Pete out the door. Together and abreast, they tramped up the hill to the hotel, in whose lobby a solitary lamp was dimly burning.

Pete held back to let Stone enter first. He followed. Their boot heels clicked on the white tile floor as they crossed to the desk.

There was a bell on it. The clerk, Hughie Smithers, was asleep behind it, his head buried in his folded arms on top of a table.

Stone turned the register and looked at it. He glanced up at Pete and shook his head. "We'll try the livery barn," he said.

Chapter 3

As Pete paced down Butte Street beside the sheriff, a kind of savage anticipation began to grow in him. He had a feeling they were going to find at least one of the strangers sleeping in the hay at the livery barn.

Sobering this growing anticipation was the feeling that if they found only one, it would probably be the one innocent of the attack. It just didn't stand to reason that a man would, after viciously attacking a girl in a strange town, remain in that town afterward. And yet if he were drunk enough it might be exactly what he'd do.

Pete's hands clenched into fists with his effort to control the murderous fury growing in him at the thought of the attacker being near. His mind kept remembering Julie, her hysterical terror, the sight of her bruised and bleeding face. Most of all he remembered the blankness that had come into her eyes at the last.

Marry her he would. On the day previously set for the wedding. But though he had little experience with women, he instinctively knew it would be a long, long time before she could be a wife to him. He scowled furiously. He loved her and wanted her desperately. Now he would have to wait.

The livery barn was a towering yellow frame structure with storage for fifty tons of hay in the loft. It would be almost gone now. The loft would be virtually empty.

The huge front doors gaped open. A smell of manure and horses and hay wafted out the door on a breeze blowing through the barn. Pete could hear the sleepy movement of horses stirring in their stalls.

Stone said softly, "Wait here. I'll talk to Bruhn."

Pete waited by the huge front door, straining his eyes into the darkness of the place. Looking through the barn he could see the square of light formed by the gaping rear doors. If anyone went through those doors he would see him.

He heard Stone open the door of the tack room, a few moments later heard Cass Bruhn's sleepy voice. Stone returned, walking softly. "Cass says he let a stranger bed in the loft tonight. He's up there now. Take this lantern and light it. I'll go up this ladder. You take the one in the rear."

Up above, the smell of hay was stronger and there was a dusty smell not present down below.

Pete peered into the cavernous shadows. His muscles and nerves were tight as fiddle strings. He held the lantern bail in his left hand, leaving his right hand free. From the front of the loft Stone

28

roared, "All right you! Come out of it with your hands in the air!"

For a long minute there was no response. Pete's hand was like a claw. He wanted to kill a man right now and, he realized with rueful chagrin, he didn't care as much as he should whether the man was proved guilty or not. A scratch on his face would have been enough to convict him in Pete's mind right now. And that was no way for a lawman to feel.

His eyes caught movement about halfway to the front of the loft. He saw a man come erect from a pile of dusty hay.

The man brushed at his clothes, then scratched his ribs. He bent and started to pick something up, probably his hat or boots, but Pete's sharp voice froze him where he stood. "Hold it, damn you! Or I'll cut you down!"

From opposite ends of the loft, he and Stone advanced, both carrying their lanterns in their left hands. The man looked with bewilderment first at Pete and then at Stone.

He was about Pete's height, but thinner and more gaunt. His clothes were both dirty and ragged, and now were littered with dry hay stems and leaves. His hair was tousled, long and uncut. He needed a shave badly and he probably needed a bath much worse.

Stone's voice was harsh and cold. "Got a gun, mister?"

The man shook his head. Pete asked in an equally harsh voice, "What's your name?"

29

"Hellman. Jim Hellman."

Pete held his lantern aloft and stared into the unshaven face. He was looking for scratches and he found one, nearly hidden beneath the growth of whiskers on the man's right cheek.

Fury boiled up in him. With his right hand he seized the man's shirt front. "You son of a bitch, where'd you get that scratch?"

Surprise touched Hellman's eyes. And the beginnings of fear. His hand went up to touch the scratch on his cheek. He said, "Brush. I . . ." He stopped and swallowed. "It's a brush scratch."

"Or a woman's fingernail, you dirty bastard!"

Stone said, "Pete!"

The fear in Hellman's eyes increased. "Wait a minute. What am I supposed to have done?"

Pete released him. He knew if he didn't he'd drop the lantern and try to kill the man. Stone said gruffly, "Come on, Hellman."

"What for? For Christ's sake, what for?"

"Come on."

Stone gave Hellman a little push toward the front of the loft. For an instant, Pete thought the man would turn and fight and he hoped fiercely that he would.

But Hellman changed his mind and shuffled toward the front of the loft. Pete picked up his boots and hat and followed.

Stone went down the ladder first. Hellman followed. Pete tossed down the boots and hat, then climbed down himself.

Hellman was sitting on a barrel, pulling on his

boots. Both of his socks had holes in them and his toes stuck out. He got the boots on and crammed his hat down on his head. Stone gave him another push and he shuffled ahead of them and out the door.

Pete felt balked and more furious because he did. Hellman wasn't the type of man he'd been looking for. Pete had looked for cruelty, arrogance, bestiality that would explain the attack on Julie tonight. In this man he found only defeat.

They reached the jail. Pete stood a few feet behind Hellman, watching him, while Stone went in to light the lamp. When he had it going, Hellman went in and Pete followed.

Pete blew out his lantern. He did likewise with the one Stone had been carrying. He closed the outside door.

"Now then, damn you, talk! Where the hell you been all night?"

Hellman looked from Pete to Stone and back again. "Right there in the loft. Since ten o'clock."

"Bruhn see you go up?"

"The stableman? Sure he did. He made me give him all the matches I had."

Pete said harshly, "And before that?"

"The saloon. The Butte."

"Drinkin'?"

The man's face flushed slightly. "A beer. I only had a nickel. I bought a beer and ate at the free lunch counter."

"How long since you had a woman?"

The man stared at the floor as he replied. "A

31

long time. What woman'd want a man like me?"

"Hold out your hands!"

The man held them out, palms up.

"Turn 'em over."

Hellman did. Pete peered closely at the knuckles, looking for abrasions that might have been caused by striking Julie's face or teeth. But there weren't any.

Not that their absence proved anything. Stone said, "Lock him up."

Pete jerked his head toward the barred door. "Go on. Move!"

The man stiffened. "Wait a minute, damn it. What am I supposed to have done? What're you juggin' me for?"

Pete started to reply, but Stone broke in. "Vagrancy will do for now. Get back there in a cell."

The stiffening in Hellman wilted. He shuffled ahead of Pete, back into the cells, and entered one of them. Pete clanged shut the door, turned the key in the lock and carried it up front where he tossed it down on the sheriff's desk.

Stone looked at him and shook his head. "Huh uh. I don't think so."

Pete went to the door and stared angrily outside. He turned abruptly and looked at Stone. "There's half a dozen men out there."

Stone got up and came to the door. He peered through the tiny door glass, which was screened and barred heavily on the inside. Pete said, "They're just standing there, watching the jail."

Stone didn't reply. He yanked open the door

and his voice, calling into the street, was harsh. "I thought I told you to go home and go to bed."

"You got him, ain't you, Jess?"

"We got a man, that's all. I don't think he's the one. Now go on home."

"You don't mean that, Jess. You know damn well it's the one."

"No I don't know it. Tomorrow, I'll question him some more. If he's clean, I'll turn him loose."

A voice yelled, "I saw you bring him in! He's the one, all right!"

Stone said sarcastically, "I'm going to get you put on the county payroll, Pomeroy. With you around, think of all the money they'll save. They won't need judges or juries anymore." He backed into the office and slammed the door. He shot the bar into place.

Pete stared at the door, thinking that this was probably the strongest jail for five hundred miles. Built of native stone, its walls were two feet thick. Log beams, hand-hewn to square them, supported the roof and not a one of them was less than fourteen inches thick. The floor was of stone blocks two feet square. There wasn't a man alive that could pry one loose.

The bars on the windows were an inch in diameter, three inches apart and anchored in the stone itself. The front door, the only door, was built from oak planks two inches thick. Nobody was going to storm this jail. Not unless there was consent within.

Pete glanced around at the clock. It said two

o'clock. In an hour it would be light enough to trail. He said, "One of us has got to stay here. I'd like to be the one to go, Jess, if it's all the same to you."

Jess Stone shrugged. "Don't see why not. I guess you've got that much coming to you."

"Thanks."

"Want a posse?"

Pete hesitated only a moment. Then he shook his head. "I'll have enough to do without worrying about a posse." He glanced at the door, thinking of the men outside working themselves up into a lynching mood.

"Suit yourself." Stone was silent for several moments. When he spoke, it was almost reluctantly. "Old Jake took it on himself to judge and execute a man. That's what broke him in the end, being wrong just once. Don't make the same mistake."

Pete stared steadily at him. Right now he didn't understand himself. A while ago he wanted to kill Hellman when he saw that scratch on Hellman's face.

What he would do when he came up face to face with the other man he didn't know. When he did know, he'd know something else as well. He'd know whether he was fit to be sheriff when Stone retired or not.

He said, "I'll go down to the stable and saddle up a horse."

Stone nodded. Pete went out. He heard Stone bar the door behind him and that, more eloquently than words could have done, told him that Stone took the group in the street seriously.

Pomeroy yelled. "Where you going, Pete?"

"To get a horse."

"Gettin' up a posse?"

"Nope. I'm going out alone."

Someone in the group laughed. Another said, "He's old Jake's kid all right."

Pete walked down Butte toward the livery barn. They expected him to come back the way Jake almost always had — with the fugitive slung dead across the saddle of his horse.

And maybe he would. He didn't know. Julie's words were ringing clearly in his mind right now. "Kill him, Pete. Find him and kill him."

That was what Julie wanted. It was what the town wanted. It was what Pete Chaney wanted himself.

He got a big brown gelding at the stable, a horse he knew had more speed and staying power than any other horse in town. He saddled him carefully, mounted and rode back to the jail. By the time he reached the place, there was a faint line of gray above the eastern plain.

He went in, selected a rifle and took two boxes of shells for it. He got an extra box for his .44. He got his roll of blankets and slicker.

He went back out and tied them on his saddle. The group still stood across the street, staring reluctantly at the jail. One of the men had a bottle and was passing it around.

Pete mounted and rode up Butte to Julie's house. It was still dark. He turned reluctantly and rode

35

to Doc's. There was a light in Doc's kitchen so he went around and knocked at the back door.

Doc was getting breakfast. "Come on in and eat."

Pete went in. Doc poured him a cup of coffee and Pete gulped it gratefully. At last he asked the question that was burning in his mind. "How is she, Doc? Is she going to be all right?"

Doc nodded, his mouth full of flapjack. He got up and flipped the one on the stove. It was about ten inches across. He said without turning, "I gave her a sedative. When she wakes, it'll be a bit easier than it was before. She's hurt and she's had a shock. The hurts will mend a hell of a sight sooner than the shock will."

"We won't have to put off the wedding, will we?"

Doc stared at him briefly, then looked away. He said, "Puttin' it off would be the worst thing you could do to her. Marry her, boy, but don't expect much right at first. Just don't expect too much."

Pete finished, thanked Doc and got up and went outside. It was light enough to see the ground. It was light enough to trail.

Chapter 4

Pete Chaney rode down Butte to the hotel. There was a predawn chill in the air and the town was gray and cheerless. He saw a light in the hotel kitchen and rode around to the rear door.

From the cook he got some supplies to take along — coffee, bacon, flour, dried fruit. He put them into a sack and tied them on behind his saddle. He mounted again and rode down Butte and out of town. The men who had been waiting in front of the jail were gone — probably to the hotel for coffee, he guessed.

It wasn't going to be easy, picking up a trail, and it would be mighty easy to choose the wrong one. Still, maybe it wasn't going to be as hard as he expected. The man he was after would likely be going at a pretty fast clip — faster than that of the average man just leaving town.

Butte Street narrowed to a road at the edge of town, crossed Rustler Creek over a bridge, turned right and headed south. Beyond the bridge, Pete swung down and peered closely at the road.

There were many tracks in the deep, dry dust, but Pete was no novice at finding trail. After several moments he selected a single set of prints, those of a horse being ridden hard.

The light was growing stronger. The east was touched with rose. He mounted again, frowning with concentration. Not that the prints were hard to see. But it was hard to keep them separated from the dozens of others covering the well-traveled road.

He rode for about a mile before the set of prints turned off. After that it was easier and he urged his horse on at a faster clip, hoping as he did that he was following the right trail.

The rose-gold color in the eastern sky increased. At last Pete dismounted again and squatted, studying the set of prints.

They were several hours old, he guessed. The time was right, if they belonged to the horse of the man he sought.

They told Pete that the man had slowed from his first hard-riding pace. That would be right too. The man would be hurrying as he left the town because of the thing he had done. But he couldn't ride that way forever unless he wanted to kill his horse.

Beyond that, there were few distinguishing features. The horse's shoes were worn. The rear feet appeared to have been shod most recently, but even these showed wear at the rear of the shoes, as though the horse had been traveling downhill over rocky ground.

A trail was like a face, Pete thought. If you had to describe it, you'd probably do so in such a way that the description could cover a hundred trails. Yet if you'd seen it yourself, if you'd studied it and knew it, you would never confuse it with another.

Satisfied, he swung astride his horse and headed out again. There was something else this trail would tell him before he reached its end. It would tell him whether the man who made it was riding openly as an honest man would, or whether he was trying to hide it in expectation of pursuit.

The sun rose in the east. This was flat and empty plain, broken occasionally by buttes similar to Gray Butte, rising like sentinels on the far horizons. And by bluffs guarding some near-dry stream.

Pete knew the country like he knew the back of his hand. There were no towns for a hundred miles in this direction. The land rose slowly and steadily during the next fifty or sixty miles until it crossed a low pass in rough and broken country covered with cedars and piñon pine. It dropped, then, crossed a wasteland almost earning the name of desert and dropped again into the valley of Shoshone Creek. Pete knew he had to catch his man before he reached Shoshone Creek or risk losing him forever.

His eyes were cold as winter ice. There was nothing easygoing about the expression on his face. Today he was a hunter, who rode with hate.

He realized that he was hoping the man he followed would try to hide his trail. He wanted to find these indications of guilt.

Yet he also realized that the man might be so sure the girl he had attacked would conceal her shame that he would not even bother to hide his trail.

Pete grinned unpleasantly to himself. He was doing something no lawman should ever do. He was trying the man in his mind as he rode. And, like a prosecutor, he wanted a guilty verdict.

What would he do when he caught up? He searched his soul for the answer to that and he found no answer no matter how he searched. He didn't know what he'd do. A lot would depend, of course, on what the fugitive did. If he fought . . . Pete would probably kill him. If he surrendered . . .

He made himself think of Julie — of the way she had come to him last night. She had turned to him when the distance home was shorter than that to the sheriff's office.

She depended on him and she had asked him to avenge the attack. He shook his head angrily, for a voice in some deep recess of his mind kept asking a nagging, unwelcome question. "What if this is not the man?"

He might not be. Hellman, confined in jail at Gray Butte, might be the one.

And again that nagging voice, with a different question now. "Do you have the right to decide which is the guilty one? What if you make a mistake?"

The trail was not easy to follow, nor did it grow

easier as the miles flowed steadily behind. Where there was rocky ground, the trail swerved toward it and became that much harder to follow. A couple of times it swerved into a trail left by cattle or horses as they made their way across the dry plain to water. The man was no fool and he was as experienced at hiding trail as Pete was at following it. That business of following a cattle trail, for instance, knowing his tracks would be wiped out the first time a bunch of cattle traveled it.

Pete's expression now was one of frowning concentration as he tried to decipher the trail and still make speed enough to catch up with his man before he reached Shoshone Creek.

Thoughtfully, he estimated the speed the fugitive was maintaining. He estimated his own. And he realized how wide was the gap between the two.

The fugitive had a start of several hours — about five to be exact. He was unhampered by the need to decipher a trail and could therefore travel as fast as he wished.

His lead was increasing and would continue to increase. Pete would lose him unless he could figure some way to get ahead of him.

He scowled, trying to recall each small detail of the land ahead. And suddenly he spurred his horse.

For he had remembered that where the land dropped away to the flat, dry desert floor, there was a sheer rock bluff, through which there were no more than three narrow trails.

It was possible, of course, that the man he pursued would veer to east or west. If that happened he would get away. But if Pete kept slavishly following trail he would get away just as clean. He could travel for miles in Shoshone Creek and never leave a track.

Having made his decision, Pete pushed his horse as hard as he dared. First of all, he must eliminate the fugitive's lead, even if it meant traveling all the coming night.

But even though he had abandoned the trail, he still kept searching the ground as he rode along, trying to pick it up again.

Twice during the day he did. And each time he felt easier because his estimate of the fugitive's direction had been correct.

Noon passed, and he stopped for fifteen minutes to rest and water his horse, to chew a few mouthfuls of dried fruit and wash them down with water from his canteen. Then he went on, still pushing hard.

Up and up, in slow stages, until the country he traveled was broken sage and cedar-covered wasteland where he could be a mile from his quarry and never know it. Gradually as the altitude increased, the sage grew higher and the cedar was replaced by scrubby pine.

The afternoon dragged, hot and dry and dusty, but Pete kept urging his rapidly tiring horse ahead. By now he should have cut the man's lead in half. With any luck he'd pass him sometime in early darkness tonight.

Then, of course, he would have to decide which of the three trails leading down off the sheer rock bluff he was going to cover. And then he'd live in a torment of worry for fear he had chosen wrong.

Half an hour before sundown, he halted again. This time he built a small fire, fried bacon, then fried flour-and-water flapjacks in the grease. He made coffee and ate leisurely while his horse grazed. When he had finished, he stretched out on his back and stared up at the changing colors in the sky.

All during the day he had avoided the decision he knew he had to make and he did so now. He tried to force his thoughts into channels that would not lead directly back to his problem, but he failed. If he thought of Julie, he inevitably thought of what had happened to her. If he thought of his father, he came face to face with the decision his father had once made so disastrously and with the one he knew he must eventually make himself.

The fugitive was certainly hiding his trail. He had proved that all morning while Pete followed so closely. Yet that did not necessarily prove him guilty of attacking Julie last night. It might mean, instead, that he was on the run for some other crime committed someplace else.

Scowling and nervous, Pete got up. He killed his fire, caught and saddled his horse and coiled the lariat he had used to picket him. He mounted up and rode out south.

As he traveled, the colors in the sky were gradually replaced by varying shades of gray. The first few stars winked out and a glow in the eastern sky heralded the rising moon.

More than sixty miles lay between Pete and the town of Gray Butte now. About thirty lay ahead.

He rode at a more leisurely pace, resting his horse and his own tight-drawn nerves as well. The hours dragged slowly past.

Near midnight, he reached the bluff and could look ahead at the vast dry plain, drenched with blue-white moonlight. He had watered his horse and filled his canteen at a spring several miles behind. Now he tied his horse and settled down at the edge of the bluff to wait.

His best chance was to wait up here where he could command a good view of the entire arid plain. When his man started across it come morning he would necessarily raise a trail of dust.

He dozed, and dreamed weird, uneasy dreams. He woke several times with a start, both sweating and cold.

But he went to sleep at last and did not awake again until the sun was poking its rim above the eastern horizon.

He leaped to his feet worriedly, relaxed as he realized how early it was. He walked to the edge of the bluff and stared out across the plain.

He saw nothing, indeed had not expected to. His quarry would not be along just yet.

He had saved some of the bacon and flapjacks he had fried yesterday and he ate them now, and drank sparingly from his canteen. He made a smoke and settled down in the shade of a jack pine to enjoy it. He peered closely out across the plain again.

Nothing yet. But heat waves were already rising out there, distorting the shapes of the few scrub plants and rocks that relieved the monotony of it.

Time passed. The sun climbed across the eastern sky. Still he saw nothing move.

He began to wonder if he had been outguessed. He frowned worriedly, but he knew it was too late to do anything about it now. If the man didn't show up by noon — well, he'd just have to back-track until he found the trail. He'd have to take it up and follow it as best he could. He didn't intend to go back to Gray Butte without his man.

A blue jay scolded him. A doe and fawn wandered to within a hundred yards of him, then spooked away from the movement of his horse. The heat increased, reflected heat from the rocks and the dried-out desert below.

He saw it, then, a wisp of dust rising a couple of miles to his right. As he stared, the rider making the dust rode up out of a dry wash onto the level plain above.

Pete was on his feet. In less than a minute he was galloping through the pines toward the trail the man had used.

A fierce excitement rose in him, and satisfaction because this time when it was so important he had guessed exactly right.

Riding hard, he reached the head of the trail

45

in about ten minutes. He slid his horse into it and started down.

The man was now about three miles ahead. From the eminence of the trail, Pete stared at the plain, mapping the course he would take.

To his right there was a long, low ridge. The rider he wanted to overtake was well to the left of the ridge.

Pete doubted if it was more than twenty or thirty feet above the level of the desert plain. But it was high enough to hide a mounted man and hide the dust he made.

Accordingly, when he reached the foot of the trail, he reined right and lifted his horse to a rocking lope. This way he continued for several miles, glancing often to his left to make sure he was not observed.

When he judged he had gone far enough, he reined to the left and half a mile farther on crested the low ridge and could look beyond.

For the briefest instant he froze because he didn't see his man where he'd expected him. Then, looking back toward the towering bluff, he saw him coming, a mile or so beyond.

Pete's horse was lathered and heaving. At a walk, in plain sight, he headed toward the man.

The rider stopped. For an instant he was like a statue, staring at this man and horse who had appeared so unexpectedly out of the empty plain. Pete rode slowly toward him, giving his weary horse this time to rest. It might end up in a running chase and if it did his horse would need all the strength he had.

The fugitive altered his course to the east. Pete also altered his. The man stepped up his pace. Pete also stepped up his.

The fugitive stopped. Pete saw a puff of smoke. Dust kicked up a hundred yards in front of him. It seemed a long time after that before he heard the rifle's report.

A warning shot. A plainly spoken, "Keep your distance whoever you are."

But Pete kept on. He saw no further puffs of smoke. The man changed course again until he was heading directly east. He urged his horse to a steady lope.

Pete rode a parallel course. Because of the change of course he was no longer ahead of his man. He was a mile to his right. And keeping pace — even drawing slightly ahead.

He used this slow but steady gain to gradually angle left. And he began to grin. By midafternoon it would be over. The man was riding a played-out horse that couldn't stand a lope for very long.

Pete closed the gap between them to a half mile, then to a quarter mile. He raised a hand and bawled, "Hold it!"

He didn't know whether the words carried or not. But the gesture must have been understood. The man spurred his faltering horse.

Pete sank his spurs cruelly. His horse leaped ahead.

The man didn't try to shoot. He leaned low over

his horse's neck and rode. Gradually Pete caught up.

Again he yelled, "Pull up! You're under arrest!"

The stranger left his saddle when Pete was still fifty yards behind. He rolled, came to a stop facing Pete. His rifle came up and barked like the nasty spitting of a mountain cat.

Pete's gun was in his hand. He was less than a dozen yards from the man and closing that distance fast. He could kill him with ease and be justified because it was strictly self-defense.

Yet suddenly killing quick with a single bullet in a vital spot did not seem enough to him.

He wanted this man to pay, in pain, in suffering, what he had made Julie pay last night. Yet that was only part of it, the part he most clearly understood. There was another part. There was a sudden and very sharp memory of that last man his father had brought in dead, eyes dull and bulging because his head hung down, tongue blackened and hanging out . . .

He left his saddle, hit the ground and rolled. He heard the stranger's rifle spit at him again, this time felt the impact of the bullet burning along his calf.

He was on the man at last, raging and furious, having in this moment of realization more than his normal strength.

He seized the hot barrel of the rifle, yanked it from the man and flung it fifty feet away. He kneed the man savagely in the face as he reached for his holstered revolver and tried to rise. Following that, he seized the man's gun wrist and twisted viciously. He caught the gun as it slipped from the man's hand and brought it angrily around in a swinging arc.

It struck the man squarely on the side of the head. He collapsed to the baking sand.

Panting, Pete looked down. He felt cheated now. He staggered to his horse and got his canteen off the saddle. He took a long and tepid drink. He replaced the canteen and led his horse to the unconscious form lying on the ground. He didn't know whether he had done right or not. But he knew this one thing at last. He had done the only thing he could.

Chapter 5

Pete waited. Blood welled from a gash made by the revolver along the captive's jawline. Blood spilled from his half-open mouth. His eyes were partly open and showed through gray.

He was a younger man than Pete had expected. He judged the stranger's age at somewhere between twenty and twenty-five.

And handsome in a reckless sort of way. Unshaven and dusty now. Looking pretty beat.

From running, Pete theorized bitterly. Running from one crime to another all the time.

He stirred the man with his foot unfeelingly. "Get up, you son of a bitch!"

The man groaned and rolled, as though to protect himself. Pete nudged him again with the toe of his boot. The way he'd nudge a rattler he thought was dead. Warily. With gun ready in his hand.

The man sat up. He opened his eyes, grimaced with pain, then stared steadily up at Pete. There was hate in those eyes. He growled, "What the hell's this all about?"

"Assault and rape. You're under arrest. You're damn lucky you're not dead."

Fear touched the stranger's eyes, briefly driving away the hate. Pete said, "Go get your horse."

The man got up and shuffled toward his horse. He caught him and swung painfully astride. Pete could feel blood running down his calf. The rear of his pants leg was soaked from knee to ankle. Not much he could do about it, though. Not now at least.

He heard the rapid pound of a horse's hoofs and swung his head. His captive had mounted and was spurring his horse rapidly away.

With a muttered curse, Pete swung to his saddle. He whirled the horse and spurred away in pursuit. He stuffed the stranger's revolver in his belt and took down his rope.

A charge like assault and rape was enough to put terror into any man, he guessed. Not many guilty of that crime ever came to trial. But running would do the man no good.

He overtook the man rapidly and swung his loop. It settled neatly over the stranger's head, tightened around his upper arms and chest. Pete yanked his horse to a halt and the stranger left his saddle to thump audibly on the hot and dusty ground.

Suddenly Pete's own weariness, the sharp, burning pain in his wounded leg, his hatred and self-disgust because he hadn't been able to kill the man — these things combined to force his action. He whirled his horse and set his spurs.

The stranger scraped and jumped along the ground at the end of the rope. Pete dragged him a couple of hundred yards and stopped. He turned his horse, rode to where the man lay and stared coldly down. "Get up and get your horse. Don't try that again."

The man staggered to his feet. He fell once, but doggedly got up once more. He fought free of the rope, dropped it and Pete coiled it up. This time Pete rode behind him until he reached his horse. The man mounted with difficulty and stared at Pete with red and hate-filled eyes. Pete said, "Back to Gray Butte. Get going."

The man didn't move. He said softly, "I'll kill you, mister. I'll kill you before I'm through."

"I've heard that before. It doesn't scare me. What's your name?"

"Caine. Luke Caine."

"All right, Caine. Get moving. Back the way you came."

"What about my rifle? It cost me eighteen dollars."

"Come back for it later. If the jury turns you loose."

"Jury hell! I'll never see a jury. Not with a charge like that against me."

Pete stared at him sourly. "Maybe you're right. Know who that girl you beat up was?"

"I never touched no girl."

Pete spat the words at him. "Liar! You ought to be lyin' across your saddle dead right now. That

52

was the girl I'm going to marry a week from next Sunday."

Even with its coating of blood and dust and whiskers, the man's face visibly lost color. His eyes turned flat and scared. He said, "Deputy, it's a goddam lie. I didn't touch no girl. I swear to God, I didn't touch no girl!"

Pete didn't reply. He just stared steadily at Caine. The man was silent for several moments. His voice, when it finally came, was panicky and so low it could scarcely be heard. "You don't intend to take me back for trial. You're goin' to kill me first damn chance you get."

"Then see to it I don't get a chance. Don't try to run again. I've controlled myself so far but don't count on it being permanent. I want to kill you so much right now it's a bad taste in my mouth."

The man shifted his glance from Pete's burning eyes. He turned his horse and headed at a slow walk toward the towering bluff.

Pete followed along behind. He wasn't proud of himself for having caught the man. He didn't even like himself. Because he knew what he was doing to Julie by bringing Caine back alive.

He was forcing Caine to trial — a trial that would force Julie to testify, however briefly, a trial that would make it impossible for anyone to forget.

There had been, in addition to the wounds Pete put there himself, several scratches on Caine's unshaven face. Scratches that Julie might have made as she fought with him. Scratches that might also have been made by brush. Pete scowled blackly

53

at his prisoner's broad, sweaty back.

He remembered Hellman, lodged in the jail at Gray Butte. Caine was the meaner of the two and, making a hasty choice, he would pick Caine as the guilty one. Yet he knew how faulty that reasoning was. The mildest of men were sometimes the meanest toward helpless things — women, children, animals.

Pete was glad, suddenly, that he didn't have to choose. He didn't have to decide which of the two was guilty. That was the business of a court.

They crossed the desert at a slow walk and labored up the steep, narrow trail leading to the top of the bluff. They entered the coolness of pines and cedars, crossed the high point passing over the spine of this range of hills and began the downward leg.

At the first narrow stream, Pete watered the horses and filled his own and Caine's canteen. He made the man dismount and tied his hands. He secured the end of the rope to his own saddle horn. Then he sat down beside the stream, removed his boot and rolled up the stiffening leg of his pants.

The leg itself had been stiffening too during the hours past. He'd been favoring the leg in the stirrup, and grimacing with pain when he was forced to use it for balance.

He washed it thoroughly in the stream, gritting his teeth and losing color as he did. He ripped off the tail of his shirt for a bandage and wrapped it around the leg, tying it with the ends. The wound was, he guessed, less than a quarter inch in depth. Perhaps half an inch wide and six or eight inches long. Deep enough to hurt like hell. Deep enough to bleed a lot. But not bad enough to cripple him or even weaken him for very long.

He got up and limped to where his prisoner was. He boosted Caine to his saddle, then walked back and mounted to his own. Caine rode out and Pete followed, keeping the rope slack between them.

The miles and the hours dropped steadily behind. The sun set and the coolness of dusk came down across the land. Pete halted and made camp. He built a fire and cooked what was left of his bacon. He fried more flour-and-water flapjacks in the grease. He untied Caine so that the man could eat.

He let him finish and smoke a cigarette, then tied him up again. This time, he tied his feet as well, despite Caine's profane objections. He laid down and stared up at the clear sky and winking stars.

Sleep came to him almost immediately, but it was a wary sleep interrupted by each small noise that disturbed the night. Each time he woke, he glanced at Caine, but the man didn't seem to have moved.

He rose at dawn, built a fire and brewed coffee. He gave Caine half of the dried fruit that remained. He drank three cups of coffee while Caine drank two.

Mounted again, roped together as before, the pair rode out. And now, with time to think, Pete found himself wondering how Julie was today.

Her hurts would have eased; her face would have begun to heal. But how about the hurts that went deeper than the flesh? He stared ahead at Caine with renewed hatred in his eyes.

They would reach Gray Butte today. About midafternoon if Pete's estimate of the horses' strength was any good.

His face was grim as he thought of it. He'd find little approval for what he'd done in the town of Gray Butte. No hero's welcome awaited him. He doubted if anyone but Stone would think he had done what was right.

His wound was evidence of his chance to kill his man. It was his justification for doing so. Julie would doubt his love, perhaps hate him for making necessary what she would now be forced to do.

Near two o'clock he brought the butte behind the town in sight and at a quarter of four entered the lower end of Butte Street after plodding hollowly over the bridge. Luke Caine turned his head.

Something close to panic was in the young man's eyes. His arrogance, his assurance — both of these were gone. He was only scared now. He said, "You wouldn't have brought me in if you'd intended to let a lynch mob have me, would you?"

Pete glanced beyond him and up the street. People all along its length had stopped as though frozen, and now were staring intently at the approaching pair. Already a knot of men was forming in front of the jail. Pete said, "We'll make a run for it. When we reach the jail, slide off and hightail it for the door. Don't try anything else or by God

56

I'll let them have you. Is that clear?"

"I won't try anything else. I never wanted to reach a jail so damned bad in my whole life!"

"Then ride!"

Pete sank spurs cruelly into his weary horse's sides. Ahead of him, Luke Caine did the same. The horses pounded up Butte Street's dusty length, raising a cloud of dust behind.

People on the walks stared at them, faces hostile and filled with anger. The knot of men in front of the jail grew larger. Pete could see others running to join it.

Maybe he'd have been smarter to ride slowly and deliberately up the street the way he'd sometimes seen his father do. Daring them with contemptuous eyes to make a hostile move.

But he didn't think he would. In the first place he was too young. He hadn't the assurance of experience his father'd had.

They were moving now, coming toward him, cutting him off from the jail. He yelled, "Fall behind!"

Caine glanced around at him. His eyes were wide, scared, and his face was white beneath its covering of whiskers and dust. His mouth hung slightly open and a little drool of saliva came from one corner of it.

For the first time, Pete was fiercely glad he had brought Caine in alive. The man was as filled with terror as Julie had been. Death back there on the desert would have been the most merciful thing Pete could have given him. He was suffering now and he would continue to suffer every hour of every day until his trial. If he was found guilty, he would go on paying even after that, until the scaffold trap sprung and his neck snapped beneath the heavy hangman's knot.

He dropped back abreast of Pete. He yelled something that Pete didn't catch. Then he fell behind.

Pete held onto the rope that secured his hands. Both horses were running hard in spite of their exhaustion, in spite of the grade they had to climb.

Men in the menacing, advancing mob were now close enough to be recognized individually. And Pete could see their expressions.

They had been working themselves up to this ever since he'd been gone. Balked by Stone from handling Hellman, they were now determined that this one should not escape their wrath.

A hundred yards. Seventy-five. Fifty. They formed a solid barrier between him and the jail.

He could feel the hot breath of Caine's horse close behind on his left side. He raked his horse's sides with his spurs and loosed an angry yell.

Twenty yards. Ten. And then he was on them and saw their faces grow scared as they realized he did not intend to stop. Again he raked his horse to forestall his stopping of his own free will.

He felt his horse's shoulder strike something solid and heard a high yell of pain. A man went rolling, taking two others down with him as he did.

Hands snatched for Pete's bridle and he slashed at them with the knotted end of the rope. A shot roared out, the bullet whistling close above his head.

Then he was through, and Caine was through, and the members of the mob were turning, their faces ugly and outraged.

Pete swung to the street before his horse had stopped, holding the rope that secured his prisoner's hands, letting the horses go on.

He ducked aside to avoid Caine's horse. He saw the sudden expression of hope cross the man's contorted face, and saw his spurs sink in.

Caine's horse leaped ahead. Pete made a turn, bringing the rope around underneath his rump. He braced himself against the impact he knew was going to come.

The rope snapped taut, singing like a fiddle string. Pete was yanked, sliding, for several feet. Then the rope went loose and slack.

Caine flew through the air like a limp rag doll thrown up by a petulant, angry child. He was all flying arms and legs, a high, wavering cry. Then he struck the ground with an ugly, sodden crash.

Pete glanced around at the mob, now coming on again. Dust boiled up around him. His teeth gleamed white against his sun-blackened, dusty face.

He heard the door of the jail. He saw Stone on the threshold, a shotgun in his hands.

He put his hands beneath the unconscious

Caine's arms and dragged him in. Stone backed after him, slammed and barred the door. Pete felt drained and tired and sick. He sank into the sheriff's chair and stared emptily at the door.

Chapter 6

He sat there wearily for a long time. Outside, he could hear the cries of the mob, could hear an occasional thump on the heavy door as someone threw something at it in balked frustration.

Stone dragged the prisoner back into a cell and Pete heard the door clang shut. He said, as Stone returned, "I suppose I ought to get Doc for him. He might have a broken bone or something. That was a damned hard fall."

Stone stared at Pete's bloody leg. "What happened?"

Pete said, "I didn't have any trouble finding his trail but I knew he had too much start on me. So I cut loose and went on ahead. I waited on that bluff about eighty miles south of here and watched the desert. When I saw him I went out after him."

Stone grinned, staring at Pete with steady eyes. "You make it sound so easy. What happened to your leg?"

"Bullet burn." He saw Stone's expression

change and said defensively, "Yeah. I could have killed him and that would have pleased everybody. Only I couldn't do it. In the first place, I don't know that he's the one. Maybe it's Hellman instead. In the second place, I got to thinking that if he was the one, shooting was just too damn quick and easy a way out for him. So I brought him back."

Stone nodded, but whether the nod expressed approval or not, Pete couldn't tell. He asked anxiously, "How about Julie? Is she all right?"

"I don't know. Nobody's seen her since you left. She hasn't been out. Not that I blame her for that."

"Have you talked to Doc?"

"Sure. He says she's doing as well as can be expected. What that means I have no idea."

Pete got stiffly to his feet. Now that it was over, now that the strain was gone, his weariness seemed overpowering. He felt as though he could sleep a week. With his hand on the door he turned, gestured with his head. "Think they'll do more than yell and cuss?"

Stone shrugged. "I wouldn't try and predict a mob."

"Maybe having two prisoners here will help."

"I doubt it. The one you brought in looks a hell of a lot more likely than Hellman ever did."

Pete listened to the uproar outside. Stone said, "Don't blame 'em too damn much. Julie's pretty and she's mighty special to everyone in town. And don't expect to be very popular with them. They think you ought to have brought your man in draped across his saddle the way your old man used to bring 'em in. Don't think Julie's going to be very proud of you either."

Pete glared at him. "What about you? Did you want me to bring him in dead? You were singing a different tune when I pulled out of here."

Stone's glance met his steadily for several moments, then dropped away in confusion. He said, "I don't know. I honestly don't know. I was just thinking that it would've saved a lot of trouble all around if you had."

"What if he's not the one?"

"He resisted arrest, didn't he? That's a crime in itself."

Stone was splitting hairs and his expression told Pete he knew he was. Pete said coldly, "I have to live with this job and I have to live with the bunch out there. But I've got to live with myself, too. I'm not God and I won't act like I thought I was. I don't want something on my conscience like Jake's got on his."

"I figured that was it."

"Anything wrong with feeling that way?"

"No. I guess there's not. Go on and get the doc. Or would you rather I did it instead?"

"Think I'm afraid to face that bunch?"

Stone stared at him for several moments, then shook his head. "No. I don't think you're afraid. But your leg's hurt and you're wore down to a nub. Stay and rest while I go after Doc."

Pete shook his head. He yanked back the bar and opened the door. He stepped out and heard

Stone slam it behind him.

A thrown rock struck him in the ribs. Maybe it had been thrown at the door and not at him, but it made his anger flare up wildly. He glared at the crowd of men in the street before the door.

He glared at them individually, one by one. He couldn't know the picture he made standing there. A three-day growth of whiskers adorned his lean and dusty jaws. His eyes were red from the sun and wind and lack of sleep. His mouth was set in a savage, angry cast and his eyes were like tiny bits of ice.

And one by one their glances fell away from his. What shouts, what insults came to his ears came from the rear of the crowd.

He strode along the walk, elbowing them savagely out of his way, ignoring their grumbling. He couldn't help but limp a little but he walked as normally as he could.

A voice yelled at his back, "Julie's goin' to be real damn proud of you!"

And another, "What're you goin' to do, bawl him out an' turn him loose?"

Pete didn't answer. It made him sick to hear Julie's name shouted in anger on the streets of the town. It made him sick to realize that every man in town knew what had happened to her. How could they marry and stay here in Gray Butte with a thing like that common knowledge with everyone?

He left the mob behind, but their shouts kept ringing in his ears. He strode up Butte, hesitated at Doc's corner, then went on toward the Duquesne house. The prisoner could wait for Doc.

Halfway up the street he met Cass Bruhn coming down, leading the two horses. Cass was stumbling something and glanced at Pete sourly. Pete didn't speak. He'd had about all the disapproval he could take today. He knew how Cass felt about horses, but damn it, a lawman used a horse as hard as the man he was pursuing or he didn't catch him. It was as simple as that.

The sun was hot and the air still. The sounds of the crowd back there at the jail made a sort of angry buzz in the air. Gray Butte towered high above the town. In another few minutes the sun would sink behind it, throwing the town into shadow, and then it would begin to cool off.

He reached the Duquesne house and went up the walk. He twisted the bell and waited. After a few moments the door opened. Mrs. Duquesne stood there. She looked at Pete's face sympathetically and approvingly. Her glance dropped, taking in his dusty, sweaty clothes and his bloody leg. She said, "Come in, Pete. I'm glad you're back, and safely too. I'm glad that man is . . . I'm glad, Pete. It's an awful thing to say, but I am."

He went in and stood uncomfortably just inside the parlor door. Mrs. Duquesne called up the stairs for Julie, and after several moments he heard her steps on the stairs.

He had always been slightly uncomfortable in this house, even when he was bathed and shaved and dressed for calling on a girl. It was so spotless, so blasted tidy. . . . He hoped Julie wouldn't keep their house that way — so clean a man was afraid to sit down for fear he'd dirty up a chair.

Mrs. Duquesne tactfully disappeared toward the kitchen. Julie came into the room. She looked at him just as her mother had, with compassion and sympathy and approval. There was a listlessness in her face, though, that wasn't like her. And her voice was lifeless. "You got him, didn't you?"

He nodded.

Her eyes clung closely to his face. "He's dead, isn't he?"

For an instant he was motionless, silent. He felt guilty, as though he had done something wrong, as though he had failed himself, and Julie, and even the town itself. He shook his head. "No. He isn't dead. He's down in a cell at the jail."

She stared at him with unbelief. "I thought . . . I asked . . ."

He said patiently, "Julie, I don't know that he's the one. There were two strangers in town that night." He stared at her, wondering at the strangeness between them. Her mouth had practically healed and the swelling had gone out of it. There was a small scab on her cheekbone and her eye was still discolored. He said, "How are you, Julie? Are you all right?"

She didn't seem to hear. Almost as though speaking to herself, she said, "That means I'll have to appear in court."

"Yes."

"Unless the town . . ." She stared steadily, disconcertingly, at Pete. "They've been talking about it, you know. Ever since you left."

"Lynching? Sure. First they wanted the one we caught in Cass Bruhn's loft. Now they want the one I brought back with me. Or maybe since they don't know which of the two is guilty, they'll just hang them both! That would fix — " He stopped, realizing how much bitterness was in his voice.

He fought down his rising anger and irritability. He was tired — beat. He wasn't as reasonable as he would normally be. He said softly, "Julie, you've been hurt. The man that hurt you will be punished. And that will be an end to it. It isn't the end of the world. It needn't change your life unless you let it. You'll heal and you'll forget, and we'll be happy together exactly as we planned."

"Maybe we won't . . ." She stopped, looking up at him with frightened eyes.

Pete closed the distance separating them. He put his arms around her and pulled her close to him. "Don't say that. I'm not an executioner and I don't think you'd want to marry one."

Her body began to shake. He tilted up her face with a gentle hand beneath her chin, but there were no tears in her eyes. She cried, "I'll have to get up and tell . . . Oh Pete, I can't!"

"Maybe you won't have to."

He felt a presence behind him and turned his head. Julie's mother stood in the archway leading to the hall.

Her eyes were blazing, her face pinched and

white. "Did I hear you right, Pete Chaney? Did I hear you say that man is still alive?"

Pete nodded. He released Julie self-consciously.

Mrs. Duquesne crossed the room. Her hand swung, collided loudly with the side of Pete's face. Her voice became a shrill scream. "Get out of here! Get out, and don't come back! What kind of man are you anyway?"

Pete opened his mouth to lash back, then shut it like a trap. He looked at Julie. "I'll see you later, when — "

Mrs. Duquesne screeched, "Oh no you won't! Not while I'm alive!"

Julie nodded at him almost imperceptibly. Pete ducked around the furious woman and scooted for the door. His own anger was rising and he knew if he stayed he would say things better left unsaid.

He went out. All the way to the walk he could hear her screeching, even though the door was closed. He headed toward Doc's place, scowling blackly. He'd taken about all he was going to take from this damned town.

He walked swiftly to Doc's, caught him as he was mounting his buggy seat. He climbed up beside Bonner, grinned wearily and said, "Drive me back to the jail, Doc. And stop in to see my prisoner a minute, will you?"

"A little the worse for wear, is he?"

"A little. But not as much as this damn town would like."

Doc clucked to his horses and drove toward

Butte. He turned and drove in silence to the jail. As he was pulling through the yelling mob, he said, "Man does what his conscience tells him is right, Pete. If he doesn't, he ain't much of a man."

He drew up before the jail and got down. Pete shoved Pomeroy and another man roughly out of his way, then knocked on the door with his fist. It opened. He pushed Doc in, went in himself and pushed it shut. Somebody had his foot in the door. Pete brought his boot heel down hard on the foot and it was snatched away. He grinned sourly, slammed the door and barred it.

Doc went immediately to the cells, carrying his bag. Stone went back to let him in. When he returned, he handed Pete a piece of paper. He said, "Caine wants to send this telegram. I guess he's entitled to that. Take it down to the telegraph office, will you? Then stop and get your supper. We'll both stay here tonight."

Pete took the paper and glanced at it. It was addressed to Matthew Caine and directed to a town about two hundred and fifty miles west. It said that he was in jail and asked his brother for help.

He tucked it in his shirt pocket and went outside again. He shouldered impatiently through the crowd and headed down Butte toward the telegraph office half a block away.

He shoved the message across the counter and waited while Will Angerman sent it. Then he walked back up Butte, passing the jail on the opposite side of the street.

He went to the hotel, climbed the stairs wearily

to his room. He washed, shaved and changed his clothes. He went downstairs and found a table in the corner of the dining room, not missing the hostile stares he got from everyone he passed.

They'd like him a hell of a lot less before this thing was finished and done, he thought. They'd like him even less than they liked him now.

Chapter 7

He finished his dinner and walked, straight and furious, through the dining room and out into the night. Down in front of the jail the crowd had thinned. There were now less than a dozen men and these were mostly the ones who had no families, men who lived alone in hotel rooms or one-room shacks or who slept in the back rooms of the saloons.

Obviously, most of them had been drinking, substituting liquor for solid food. Yet there was no boisterousness among them. There was no quarrelsomeness yet. So far they were quiet, peering at Pete almost sullenly as he came down the street and entered the jail.

Once inside, he stared angrily at Stone. "By God, you'd think I'd committed some kind of crime!"

Stone grunted. "Figured it'd be that way. Told you."

"Yeah. You did, didn't you?" He turned and stared through the small door glass. It was light outside, but the sun was down behind the bluff.

The clock said a quarter of six. It wouldn't be dark for a couple of hours yet.

He went over and sat down on the cot. "Caine all right?"

"Yeah. Banged up a little is all. No broken bones."

Pete lay down on his back and put his hat over his eyes. He was so tired his head seemed to whirl. He didn't care right now what happened, just so it didn't keep him awake. You didn't get much sleep when you knew there was a trussed-up prisoner half a dozen feet from you who would kill you if he could.

He slept, and did not wake again until long after dark. The sound that woke him was the solid thump of a log against the door.

He sat up abruptly and stared around him with confused and startled eyes. Stone was standing on the far side of the room near the gunrack. But he didn't have a gun.

Pete got up. He crossed to the rack and snatched down a double-barreled ten-gauge. He crossed to the desk and got a handful of shells. He broke the gun and punched two in, then closed the action with an angry snap. He stared hotly at Stone. "What the hell's got into you? They've got a ram out there."

Stone shrugged. "I know they have. What do you expect me to do, shoot decent people that belong in this town to save a lousy rapist?"

"Decent people? Have they told you which one they want to hang? Or are they going to hang them both on the chance that one is sure to be the guilty one?"

Stone flushed with anger. He said, "Don't you talk that way to me. I'm the sheriff here. You're only my deputy."

Pete grunted contemptuously. He said, "Jake maybe made some mistakes. But he never turned a prisoner over to a lynch mob. And I'm not going to either."

"I could take away your badge. I could suspend you or even fire you."

Pete swung his head and stared at him coldly. "Don't try it, Jess."

He walked over to the door. He waited until the ram struck thunderously, then threw the bar and yanked open the door. He caught them by surprise and for an instant all were motionless.

It was a weird scene. A dozen or more lanterns lighted the street before the jail. The ram was an old telegraph pole they'd found somewhere. There were probably fifty men in the street, ten or twelve of whom were holding the ram.

Pete yelled, "Which one do you want to hang?"

"The one you brought in."

"How do you know he's the one?"

"He's the one, all right. By God he's the one. You can look at him an' tell that."

Pete grinned. "That sounds like Pomeroy."

That brought an uneasy laugh from some of them. Pete didn't wait until it stopped. His voice lashed them like a whip. "Break it up and get on home. Maybe Jess would have let you in, but

I won't! The muzzle of this shotgun is going to be six inches from the door all the rest of the night. If that ram hits it again, I'll fire through the door. It's loaded with buck, boys, and you know what it'll do to whoever's holdin' the ram."

The street quieted suddenly under the impact of his words. He stared at them harshly. Then he turned, went back inside and slammed the door. He hooked a chair with his foot, pulled it over and sat down directly in front of the door, facing it.

He looked up in time to see an unrecognizable face peering at him through the dirty door glass. It disappeared.

There'd be a lot more talk out there, he knew. There'd be some drinking and some wild threats. But nobody was going to pick up that ram again and hit the door. And without a ram they hadn't a chance of breaking in. He cocked one of the hammers and settled down to wait. He knew they'd try him before they went away. And he wouldn't disappoint them when they did.

He waited for about five minutes. He heard the cot creak behind him as Jess Stone lay down on it. He heard the prisoners talking together back in their cells, but he couldn't make out their words.

And then it came, so suddenly that even though he was expecting it, it startled him. It was a solid thump upon the door. Only it was a large rock instead of the ram.

He fired instantaneously, the muzzle of the shotgun less than six inches away from the door.

The noise, here in this confined space, was deafening. Smoke billowed from the muzzle of the gun, struck the door and spread in all directions. When it cleared, Pete could see the hole he'd blown in the door, two inches across, ragged and splintered at the edges of it. But he heard no cries of pain outside.

He broke the gun and punched a live shell in. He snapped it shut again and recocked the hammer.

Laying the gun across his thighs, he fished the makings from his shirt pocket and rolled himself a smoke. He looked around at Jess.

There would be no more trouble here tonight. Unless one of them was prepared to shoot him through the hole in the door and he didn't figure they'd go that far. Not yet at least.

Gradually the noise in the street quieted. The lanterns disappeared.

Stone slept noisily on the couch, but Pete Chaney stayed awake, staring gloomily at the jagged hole in the door so close in front of him.

He'd blown a hole in the door, but that wasn't the end of it. He had an uneasy feeling, so strong as to be almost a certainty. This business would blow a hole in the solidarity of the county and the town, just as his shotgun had blown one in the door. There was more to come — trouble, bloodshed, even death. He could almost wish now that he'd killed Luke Caine when he had the chance.

Chapter 8

At dawn, Pete got up quietly from his chair. He opened the front door and stepped outside.

The air was cool and pleasant, the street utterly silent. A dog wandered into the middle of it, sat down and scratched vigorously. He got up, saw Pete, and came toward him, wagging his tail. Pete bent and briefly petted his head. The dog waited hopefully for several moments, then trotted on up the street.

Pete thought of the things that had happened in the past few days. The attack on Julie, the arrest of Hellman, the pursuit and capture of Caine, the ugly violence that now threatened the town. So sharply were these things in contrast with the peacefulness of the street today that they seemed incredible, like parts of a nightmare from which the town would soon awake.

But it was no nightmare and was very real. It was the street and the stillness of the pleasant morning air that were deceptive. They were the things that were unreal.

He went back inside, closed and barred the door. Stone still snored noisily on the office couch. Pete stared down at him.

There had been a quality about Stone last night that disturbed him. A contradictory quality. He had not suspected Stone of either indecision or cowardice.

But perhaps it wasn't either, he thought. Any lawman would think twice before killing honest citizens in defense of a rapist, even if the rapist had not been convicted, nor even tried.

He turned away, shrugging lightly. If either weakness or cowardice was present in Stone, it would come out in the next couple of days.

He returned to the window and stared out between the stout iron bars. Perhaps he was the one that was wrong. Perhaps bringing Caine in alive when he didn't have to had been the worst mistake of all. Maybe the remorse that had marked his father and destroyed him had exerted too strong an influence on Pete himself.

He shook his head impatiently. He heard a cot creak back in the cells at the rear, and a few moments later heard Caine's voice. "Hey!"

He crossed the office and opened the door leading to the cells. There was a corridor beyond the door that ran to the rear wall of the jail. Two cells opened off each side of the corridor. Caine's was the first one on the left. Hellman, who was still asleep, was in the first one on the right.

Caine was standing at the bars, his hair tousled, his eyes clouded with awakening. He said, "When do we eat, deputy?"

Pete said sourly, "Six. It's only four-thirty. You'd just as well go back to sleep."

"Got the makings?"

Pete handed him his sack and papers. Caine rolled a smoke, then stuck the sack into his pocket. "Got a match?"

Pete handed him several matches, strong dislike apparent in his eyes.

Caine asked, "Send that telegraph message for me?"

Pete nodded.

"Sure it went out?"

"I stood there while he was sending it."

There was a subtle change in Caine's expression. Pete said, "Don't count on that brother of yours. He'd have to be a magician to get you off."

Caine grinned. He drew a lungful of smoke and exhaled it in Pete's face.

Pete's hand went through the bars, grabbed a handful of Caine's shirt front. He yanked Caine toward him violently. Caine's face struck the bars. His nose began to bleed. Pete gave him a violent shove, releasing him as he did. Caine staggered backward across the cell. He recovered and stood glowering at Pete.

Pete said, "Don't get smart with me. Rape carries a death penalty in this state and it'll take more than a brother to get you off!"

Caine swiped at his bleeding nose with the back of his hand. He said softly, "You dirty son of a

78

bitch! There's one thing I'm going to do before I leave this town."

"Kill me? I won't be hard to find."

He turned and left the cell block, kicking the door angrily shut behind. The noise woke Stone and he sat up suddenly and put his bare feet on the floor. He asked hoarsely, "What's wrong?"

"Nothing. Everything's all right. Want some breakfast?"

"Sounds good to me."

Pete said, "I'll be right back. Steak and eggs all right?"

"Uh huh."

Pete put on his hat and went out the door. He heard the bar slide into place behind him. He walked along the street toward the hotel. In front of it, a man was sweeping the porch and walk. It was someone Pete didn't know, probably a drifter passing through, working out meals and a room at the hotel. He went on in.

The dining room was deserted at this hour, but he could hear sounds of activity from the kitchen in the rear. He crossed to it and pushed open the door.

Leon Pattee, the cook, turned his head. Pete asked, "Coffee ready?"

Leon nodded. Pete crossed the kitchen and Leon handed him a steaming mug. Pete sipped it before he said, "Steak and eggs for Stone and myself. Send over a couple of trays later for the prisoners, will you?"

Leon nodded without speaking. He turned to

the stove and began to prepare the breakfasts Pete had ordered.

Pete stared at his back. Leon hadn't said anything about the arrest of Caine. He hadn't needed to. He'd looked at Pete as though he were someone he knew but couldn't understand. The joviality he'd always shown Pete before on these early morning visits was gone.

The trouble was, Pete thought, that every man in town had put himself in Pete's place. Each of them knew what he would have done. The thing that none of them had considered was that a lawman is sworn not to let personal feelings or considerations affect the conduct of his job. A lawman was supposed to be impersonal. If he wanted to live with himself he couldn't allow himself to prejudge an accused.

He shrugged lightly. To hell with it. He was doing a job, not trying to be popular. If he'd wanted approval from the townspeople, he should have killed Caine for resisting arrest.

He finished the coffee and poured himself another cup from the pot on the stove. He wandered into the dining room and sat down. It was still deserted. He fished in his pocket for makings, then remembered that Caine had kept them. He got up, went into the lobby and crossed to the deserted desk. He went behind it, got sack tobacco and papers, leaving a nickel on the desk to pay for them.

He returned to the dining room and rolled himself a smoke. By the time he had finished it, and the coffee, Pattee had the two breakfast trays ready for him.

He carried them out and back along the street to the jail. He kicked on the door and after a moment Stone opened it.

Pete carried the trays in and Stone barred the door. In silence the pair sat down and ate. When he had finished, Pete rolled himself another smoke. Stone packed and lighted his pipe.

Pete asked, "When's Judge Donahue due?"

"Couple of weeks."

Pete wished the judge were in town right now. He wished they could bring Caine to trial today. As long as they couldn't, he didn't suppose it mattered whether the judge came in two days or two weeks. The town would either quiet down or it would explode. Whichever it was going to be, it would be over in forty-eight hours.

He said, "You want to go out for anything?"

Stone shook his head. "Why?"

"I thought maybe I'd go up and see Julie."

Stone glanced at him strangely, then glanced away. He said, "Go ahead."

Pete went out. There were a few people stirring in the street now and each had an unfriendly stare for him. He walked up Butte toward the Duquesne house at its upper end.

He didn't really think much was going to happen today, but he intended to stick close to the jail anyway. No telling what Stone might do if the townspeople got insistent the way they had last night.

Probably all they'd do today was gather in groups and talk out their anger and outrage. Tonight, though, was another matter. When they started drinking tonight . . .

He reached the Duquesne house and paused a moment at the gate. He wanted to see Julie. He wanted to hold her in his arms. Most of all he wanted to know if the horror and shock had faded from her eyes.

Yet he dreaded going in as well. He dreaded the bitterness he would encounter in Julie's parents. He was afraid that Julie might be worse.

He went in the gate and up the walk. He raised his hand to knock, but the door opened before he had the chance.

Mrs. Duquesne stood framed in the doorway. Her face was white, her lips thin and pinched, her eyes snapping with hate. Her voice was almost a hiss. "Get out of here! Get out and don't come back! Julie doesn't want to see you and I can't stand the sight of you!"

Pete said, "Is it that Julie doesn't want to see me or that you don't want her to?"

"Julie wants a man, not a coward that won't protect his own. Now get out of here before I get the poker and run you off!"

Pete shrugged. He couldn't force his way into the house and he couldn't get past Mrs. Duquesne unless he did. He turned and went back down the walk. He paused again at the gate and stared at Julie's upstairs window. He thought the curtain stirred but he could not be sure.

Did Julie hate him as her mother did? He didn't know, but he thought it very possible that she did. Julie herself had said, "Kill him, Pete," and while it may have been shock and outrage speaking for her, he could not be sure. Perhaps she still felt that way. Perhaps she always would.

Walking down Butte, he felt a bleak despair. Was conscience really this important? Even if Caine was properly tried and convicted, would that prove he was the guilty one? Pete shook his head. Caine couldn't get a fair and impartial trial in Gray Butte. No one accused of raping Julie could.

Guilty or innocent, Caine would hang. So what did it matter, really, that Pete's conscience had made him bring the man in alive? Caine would die and dying by the gun was a lot easier than dying by the rope.

He hesitated a moment at the corner of his father's street. Then, making up his mind, he turned and walked along toward his father's house. It was early, but he knew Jake would be up.

As he walked, he puzzled at himself. Ever since he could remember he had gone to Jake when he was troubled or confused. Not often had Jake's advice been helpful, and often Jake had simply been unable to understand the problem itself. Yet he kept going back, and each time he hoped Jake would comprehend what was in his mind.

Asking for advice, he supposed, was always an unsatisfactory business because you seldom heard what you wanted to hear. He grinned ruefully to himself, thinking that what he really wanted was

83

approval, not advice.

There was a plume of smoke coming from the tin chimney at the rear of Jake's small house. He kicked through the weeds and walked around to the back door, which was open.

He called, "Jake?"

"Come on in."

Pete went in. The kitchen was untidy, as it always was. He got a cup from the cupboard, carried it to the stove and poured himself a cup of coffee.

Jake was sitting at the table, eating breakfast. Pete sat down across from him. He said, "Julie's mother won't let me in the house."

Jake didn't reply.

Pete stared straight at him. He asked, "Did I do right, Jake?"

Jake continued to eat, continued to stare at his plate. His hand began to tremble slightly. Pete said, "Jake?"

Jake looked up. He seemed to be fighting some kind of battle within himself. At last he said, "You did right, though there ain't going to be many that think so. You got some rough days coming up."

"I know that."

"Stone won't be any help. He'll break when the going gets rough."

Pete stared closely at him. "How did you know that?"

The old man shrugged. "I've known him a long time. He's a careful man, never goes out without a posse, never lets things get out of hand. This time he ain't going to have a choice. Things'll get bad whether he likes it or not."

"How bad, Jake? You think they'll try to break into the jail?"

Jake nodded. "They'll try."

Pete was silent for a long time. Frowning, he asked, "Would you kill people to protect a prisoner like that, Jake?"

It was Jake's turn to be silent. He said slowly at last, "There was a time when I would. Right now, I don't know. I reckon that's something you're going to have to settle for yourself. I'll tell you one thing, though. If you ever give a prisoner to a mob, you're through. It's something that will never wash away. And when it's over, it's you they'll blame because they can't stand to blame themselves."

Pete nodded. He got up. "You've been a help, Jake."

Jake's shoulders seemed to straighten a little. His eyes seemed suddenly a little clearer than they had before. He started to get up, then sank back into his chair. He mumbled, "You need anything, you let me know."

"Sure." It was as close to an offer of help as he would get, Pete knew. Yet it was more than he had expected. Not that he could count on it. Jake's grudging offer of help today might be withdrawn tomorrow. But at least, this time, Pete had heard what he wanted to hear. He had heard what he'd needed to hear if he was to go on.

Chapter 9

Pete returned to the jail, and the day wore on with almost boring monotony. Stone went home in midafternoon for his daily nap. The heat inside the jail built up steadily as the sun continued to beat mercilessly against the flat roof.

Pete sat at the sheriff's desk, leaning back in the swivel chair, his feet on the piled-up papers lying scattered there. He dozed, but a persistent fly kept waking him and he felt too indolent to get up and kill it.

Occasionally Caine would yell something from his cell in the rear of the jail, but mostly Pete ignored his demands.

The quiet in Gray Butte was deceptive, Pete knew. He got up and walked to the window. He stared outside. Other than a larger-than-usual crowd in front of both saloons, the street appeared exactly as it did any other day. Yet there was something... something about the way every passer-by glanced at the jail, something about the way the crowds in front of the two saloons talked. . . .

Trouble was brewing even though it might not break openly until darkness gave an illusion of anonymity to the men who would form the mob.

Pete turned and wandered across to the gunrack on the wall. He took down a double-barreled shotgun and broke it absently. It was the same gun with which he had blown a hole in the door last night. It was the gun he would use tonight.

There is terror in a shotgun for most men, probably because of the awful damage it can do at close range, perhaps also because with a shotgun it is virtually impossible to miss.

He wondered if he was capable of firing into a mob to protect a prisoner. It was something he'd find out, he supposed, but he doubted if he'd know for sure until the time for it actually came.

The sun dropped behind the butte to the west of town, and in shadow, the air began to cool. Stone returned at five-thirty. Pete unbarred the door for him. Stone shoved back his hat, mopped his broad forehead with a sleeve and said, "Go ahead and eat."

"All right. I won't be long."

"Take your time. Nothin's going to happen yet."

Pete glanced closely at the sheriff's face but it was bland and almost bored, as though this were just another ordinary day. He went out and closed the door behind him. He did not hear the bar slide into place.

He hesitated for a moment, then walked away. Stone would bar the door. He just hadn't done it immediately, that was all.

Pete walked toward the hotel, savoring the coolness of the air after the stuffiness of that inside the jail.

He went into the hotel and ordered his supper, then sat by the window waiting for it and staring into the street. It was almost too quiet, he thought. Too ordinary. There should have been some yelling down at the saloons. There should have been a few truculent drunks clustered in front of the jail.

Uneasiness began to grow in Pete. Then Sally Pattee brought his tray and he put his attention on his food. He noticed that Sally had given him that "looks like a decent woman isn't safe in this town any more" look before she went away, and grinned ruefully to himself. If anybody had bothered to think about it they'd know that an arrest, a trial, a conviction and hanging would be much more effective deterrents than a lynching by a mob. But no one was going to admit it now.

He glanced out the window again. Light was fading, but the sun wouldn't really set for some time yet.

He finished his dinner and sipped his coffee. Abruptly, then, he gulped the last of it and got to his feet. He dropped a quarter on the table and hurried outside. Jake had said if he needed anything . . . and Jake was a symbol to the people of this town. He was a symbol of law — of ruthless and uncompromising law of the gun.

Jake had been a broken man for several years.

But enough of the people remembered him as he once had been for him to be an effective deterrent against any organized attempt to storm the jail.

Besides, Pete didn't think Stone was going to hold out very determinedly. The way Stone was acting, he might sell out pretty cheap. But with three of them, Jake, Stone, himself . . . maybe the jail would hold.

He walked up Butte and turned toward Jake's house. Once or twice he glanced behind and wondered at himself because he did. He was getting jumpy, he thought.

Half a block short of Jake's house he saw three men come from either side of the street and stand blocking it in the middle. His feeling of uneasiness increased. He glanced behind, saw four others silently walking along the street behind him.

Now he understood his nervousness. It hadn't been imagination at all. They'd been watching him ever since he left the jail. If they hadn't caught him here, they'd have caught him between the hotel and the jail.

He was the one that stood between Caine and the people of the town. Without him, they could have Caine any time they wanted him.

He glanced around. He supposed he could still run. They might have the alley between here and the jail covered, in fact they probably did. But if he ran, there was a good chance he could get away.

Only he wouldn't run. If he ran now his authority and influence would be gone.

He paced steadily ahead. The group in the middle of the street moved out of it and blocked the walk.

Pete's mind raced. He would get no help from Jake. Jake's house was over half a block away and his hearing wasn't as good as it used to be. Unless there were gunshots, Jake probably wouldn't hear a thing.

Nor could Pete expect any help from Stone. Stone was inside the jail and wouldn't leave no matter what he heard for he certainly was aware that the minute he left the townsmen would come after Caine.

Pete had his gun. He could draw it and threaten the men confronting him. But he knew, and they would also know, that he wouldn't shoot. He wouldn't kill a man unless it was in defense of his life. He couldn't know whether he was defending his life or not until it was too late.

Only fifty feet now separated him from the six. Behind him, the other four had drawn closer, almost eagerly.

He kept walking, his pace as inflexible as his eyes. Stopping would be the worst thing he could do. It would hand the men confronting him the initiative. It would tell them he was afraid.

The distance dwindled to thirty feet, to twenty-five. Still he kept walking, his eyes as hard as the gray ends of bullets peering from the cylinder of a gun.

One of them fidgeted, as though to step aside. For an instant it looked as though they might break ranks and let him through.

But behind him, the gravelly sounds of feet in the street speeded as the four broke into a lunging run. One of them yelled, "Nail him! Nail the bastard and then we'll get that lousy rapist and string him up!"

Only five feet . . . but it might have been five hundred yards. The six stood firm.

Pete reached them and roughly shouldered through. At almost the same instant one of the running four struck him bodily from behind.

He drew his gun as he fell, and twisted his body as he hit the walk. He brought the gun down on the head of the man who had knocked him down.

The man slumped and released his hold. But it was too late now for Pete to get up. Kicks and blows rained on him. He felt one of his ribs crack under the pointed toe of a boot.

He seized the pair of legs nearest him and brought the man crashing to the walk. By sheer will power, he fought to his knees.

A swinging revolver barrel cracked against his right forearm, numbing it instantly, making it impossible for his fingers to continue grasping the gun. It clattered noisily to the boardwalk and was kicked away.

Disarmed now, he thought. Helpless. Impossibly outnumbered. But God damn them, they weren't going to get away with it.

He drove forward and up, his legs pumping like pistons beneath him. He struck a man and bowled him aside. He struck another and elbowed him savagely in the throat. The man began to choke and gasp.

Pete drove through into the clear, nearly falling from his own unimpeded momentum. He whirled to face them again.

He could still run, and perhaps now they would let him go. One of their number lay unconscious on the ground. Another was choking and retching, bent half double with pain and clutching his throat. Still a third stood apart, hunched, pain twisting his face.

Pete's breath came in hoarse gusts. He wouldn't run. Damn them, they couldn't make him run.

They advanced on him in a semicircle, cautiously. He backed, circling as he did, thinking that if he could get a wall at his back he might have a better chance.

They sidled, crabwise, to cut him off. His anger mounted. These were men he knew, respectable men of the town for the most part. Between his clenched teeth he panted, "Bastards! Break it up and go home. You think you want to hang Caine, but do you know how you'll feel when you see him dangling from a rope? Do you know how you'll feel the next day and the day after that?"

They hesitated and with a sudden rush he made it to the building and got it at his back. An enraged voice shouted, "What kind of lily-livered bastard are you, Chaney? If somebody raped my wife . . ."

Disgust ran strongly through Pete. There was no reasoning with them, and he'd just as well stop trying. He said, "Come on then, damn you! Let's get this over with."

Something about their faces — their eyes . . . they were not the men he knew, the storekeepers, the others. They had changed. All had been drinking but it was not liquor that put such a peculiar light in their eyes, that twisted their mouths and flushed their skins.

They moved in, slowly, cautiously but inexorably. From five feet one of them slammed into Pete, swinging a vicious right, raising a knee immediately afterward to catch him in the groin.

His own fist slammed against the man's cheekbone with a sodden crack. His other fist doubled the man with a savage blow to the belly.

But the man had made an opening for the others. He slumped at Pete's feet to be trampled by the others as they lunged in.

It was cut and dried as Pete had known it would be. His own blows landed but they were absorbed and seemed to have no appreciable effect. His assailants' blows, concentrated as they were, made a pulp of his face, doubled him with excruciating pain in his midsection, and at last beat him by sheer force into the ground again.

He knew instinctively that he would not make it to his feet a second time for there was now an appalling savagery about the way they kicked and beat at him. One had a board pried from the walk, and struck him with it repeatedly. Pete Chaney's senses began to fade.

He remembered fury greater than anything he

had ever known. He remembered crawling along the ground trying to get clear so that he could rise again. Not for an instant did he consider anything but continuing to fight until he could fight no more.

But tough as he was, unyielding as he was, he could only stand so much. A curtain of blackness descended over his eyes and he lay as though dead in the deep, dry dust of the street.

The men surrounding him stopped, looked dazedly at each other's faces, turned and shuffled exhaustedly away. They had accomplished their purpose. Pete Chaney was unable to defend the jail. There was no hurry now for what they meant to do.

Pete lay alone in the dust while light slowly faded and the sky turned gray. . . .

His first awareness was that someone was shaking him, tugging at him, talking to him in excited tones. He fought for consciousness but it was several long minutes before he could open his eyes and focus on the face so near his own.

Jake's face. Then Jake had heard and come in time. The sky was almost wholly dark, yet enough light lingered to make his father's outline plainly visible against it.

Jake's voice was thick with anger. "The dirty bastards! God damn it, boy, get up on your feet. I'll take you home and wash you up and then by Jesus Christ, the two of us are going down there and show this town a thing or two!"

Helped by his father, Pete fought stubbornly to his feet, gasping with the pain of doing so. He leaned heavily on Jake and limped toward Jake's house. He had gone fifty yards before he said, "My gun. I want my gun."

"All right. All right. I'll get it." Jake left him and he stood alone, swaying, until Jake found the gun and returned. Then, together, they continued with agonizing slowness until they reached Jake's house.

Pete sank into a chair. Jake pulled the cork from a whiskey bottle and brought it to him. He said, "Take a drink. Take a damned big drink."

Pete did. He gagged, but the liquor warmed his stomach and revived him a little. Jake took the bottle and soaked a rag with whiskey from it. He mopped Pete's face with the reeking rag.

Every cut was like a fire, but the pain cleared Pete's head. Jake finished and said, "Break any bones?"

"Maybe a rib, but I can worry about it later. Let's get down to the jail before it's too damned late."

He stood up, swayed until his head cleared, then stumbled toward the door. Jake, following, said, "You're tough. If they haven't already strung him up I think the two of us can put a crimp in them."

Chapter 10

Walking was torture for Pete. Every muscle had absorbed kicks and blows from the men who had attacked him, so every small movement hurt. Breathing was equally painful because of the broken rib. He breathed with short, shallow gusts, which made it seem easier.

They walked along Jake's street, past the place where the attack had taken place. Pete felt his anger rising as they did. He said, "For God's sake, Jake, what gets into them?"

"The devil," Jake replied shortly.

"Have you ever seen a mob before?"

"Once."

"Here in Gray Butte?"

"No. It was down in New Mexico."

"What happened?"

Jake's voice was bitter. "What usually happens? They hanged a man from the flagpole out in front of the hotel. They said he'd killed a girl." Jake shrugged in the darkness. "I don't know whether he did it or not. Nobody ever knew. He screamed and bellered until he choked that he hadn't done it."

"What about the people that lynched him?"

"The law didn't punish 'em, if that's what you mean. But I reckon they punished themselves. The body hung there for three days because nobody would cut it down."

Pete heard a kind of wordless roar from the direction of the jail. It came faintly on the evening air and could be only one thing: the shouting of many voices. He said, "Hurry up."

He yanked his revolver from its holster and thumped it against his hand to loosen any dirt that might have gotten into it. He lifted it and blew into the barrel. That was clear, at least.

He said, "They figure they got rid of me and they know Stone won't hold out very long."

He hurried, in spite of the increased pain. Jake kept pace beside him. Pete said, "I hope we get there before it's too late."

He could feel Jake staring at him. "Think you can shoot into 'em if it comes to that?"

Pete snorted bitterly. "You're damned right I can. An hour ago I didn't think I could, but I know better now."

"Because they roughed you up?"

Pete shook his head, then said thoughtfully, "Not because they roughed me up. I guess because I saw their faces while they were doing it."

They swung around the corner onto Butte. Pete could see them now, a black and angry mass clustered around the jail like flies around a carcass in the sun. A few of them held lanterns. Because Pete and Jake were closer now, their shouting seemed louder and more insistent. Individual voices were occasionally audible. "Stone! God damn it, open up! Your deputy ain't around to help you out. You're all alone. Open up before we knock the door apart!"

There was no reply from the jail. Its windows were dark. Pete could imagine Stone standing inside in the darkness, hesitating between leaving the door barred and opening it. He could imagine the two prisoners in the cells. Caine's arrogant self-assurance would be gone. There would be sheer terror in his eyes.

Pete grinned humorlessly. Thinking of Caine in terror pleased him even though he intended to see to it Caine wasn't lynched. Again he realized how easy it would have been for Caine if he had killed him out there on the plain. This way, Caine was suffering as he had made Julie suffer. And he'd go on suffering until the trap was sprung.

There was little more than half a block between them and the jail right now. Pete was walking as fast as he could and because of his rapid movement the pain was nearly unbearable.

Until now he had not noticed what kind of gun Jake had. Now he did. It was a scarred, battered ten-gauge, doublebarreled. He glanced aside at Jake's face, visible now in the faint light from half a dozen lanterns held by individuals in the crowd.

Jake's face was not that of a broken man. His eyes were narrowed and intent. His mouth was a thin and angry line.

Pete asked, "Got more shells?"

"Uh huh."

"Then give 'em one barrel over their heads."

Jake lifted the muzzle of the gun. He fired. Smoke belched from the muzzle of the gun. The sound of the charge was like a sudden rush of wind. Shot rattled against buildings farther down the street, and there was a tinkle of glass from a broken upstairs window. Pete bawled, "Move back into the middle of the street!"

They turned to face the advancing pair but nobody obeyed. Pete yelled, "Move!"

Still the mob stood, sullen and hesitating. Someone yelled, "Don't listen to him! After what we done to him he ain't no more'n barely standin' up. An' Jake . . . well hell, you all know what Jake is!"

Pete said, "Put the other barrel into that building across the street, just barely over their heads. And then reload."

Jake turned slightly. This time he brought the shotgun to his shoulder. He fired, and again the black-powder smoke billowed from the muzzle of the gun. The shot rattled against the building across the street and again glass tinkled from broken windows.

Jake wasted no time. The report had scarcely stopped reverberating before Jake had broken the gun and punched in two live shells. He closed it with a snap.

Pete bawled, "Now God damn it, move back

into the middle of the street! The next one will be right in the middle of you! Maybe the ones in back won't get hurt, but those in front sure as hell will."

He and Jake were now less than ten feet from the nearest members of the crowd. Pete shouted, "You! And you! Know what a charge of buck from a ten-gauge does to a man this close?"

The men in front began sidling to right and left. Those immediately behind, finding themselves exposed, also began to fade to right and left.

In ten seconds the boardwalk in front of the jail was clear. By the time Pete and Jake reached the door, they had all moved back into midstreet.

Pete kicked on the door, puzzled because it opened before the force of his kicks. He pushed Jake in, went in himself, closed and barred the door behind him. He said, "Light a lamp, Stone."

There was no reply. Pete holstered his gun, fumbled for a match and struck it against the wall. He didn't see Stone so he crossed to the desk and lighted the lamp. He looked around again. He said, "Stone must be with the prisoners."

He hadn't given Stone enough credit, he guessed. If the man was back with the prisoners it meant he intended to defend them. If he'd meant to turn them over to the mob, he'd have been in here.

He walked back and opened the door. He struck another match. Holding it high, he saw Caine in one cell, Hellman in the other. The faces of both were white and scared. But Stone wasn't there.

He returned to the office, closing the door behind him. He felt a little sick. Stone had been ready to sell out cheap. When Pete and Jake showed up and diverted the mob's attention, he had ducked out of the door and left. No telling where he was now.

Pete scowled, disturbed over how wrong he had been about Stone. He'd always thought Stone was tough and competent, until lately at least when he'd begun to suspect that he was neither. He said, "Stone ran out."

"Figured he had when we found the door unlocked."

Pete lighted two more lamps. Taking the shotgun from the rack and loading it, he went to the door and opened it. He stepped out and immediately moved to one side of the door so that the light could shine into the street. He yelled, "You'll need guts to take this jail tonight. If you've got enough, come take it now. Or get liquored up first and then come with your stinkin' battering ram. But don't expect me to hesitate after what the bunch of you did to me a while ago. The first five inside the jail will be dead. Any time five of you are ready to die for Caine, come after him!"

He backed into the doorway and kicked the door shut behind him. He slammed the bar into place.

He leaned the shotgun against the wall beside the door. Outside, he could hear shouting voices, unrecognizable because of the muffling effect of the thick door and walls of the jail.

He went over and sat down on the cot. He

glanced up at Jake with a rueful smile. "I feel like hell. This is going to be a damned long night."

"Maybe not. I think they'll go home now."

Pete shrugged. "I hope you're right. I feel like I could sleep a week."

He knew that one thing and one thing only had stopped the mob out there. They had believed him when he said Jake would shoot straight into them. They believed Jake capable of it. They had also believed him when he said the first five inside the jail would be dead before the sixth got in.

He closed his eyes wearily. He wished he could sleep a few moments. If he could, maybe some of the aches and pains in his body would go away. Maybe his head would clear again.

He didn't remember going to sleep. He snapped awake with a terrifying feeling of impending disaster. He sat up, then winced and grunted with the pain of it.

But everything was all right. The lamps were still burning; the door was still closed. Jake was sitting at the desk.

He saw that Pete was awake and got up. The chair creaked. Pete realized suddenly that everything was quiet outside. He said, "They're gone?"

"Uh huh. Been quiet for an hour now."

"How long did I sleep?"

Jake pulled out his watch. "Couple of hours."

"Heard from Stone?"

"Not a word."

Pete asked, "Do I smell coffee?"

"Yeah. Sit still. I'll get you a cup."

Jake went over to the small, pot-bellied stove in the corner. He poured a cupful from the pot sitting on top of it. Pete realized he was sweating. He fished for makings and began to roll a smoke.

Jake brought him the coffee and he sipped it gratefully. He heard hoofbeats rattling in the street and heard them stop in front of the door.

He glanced at Jake, then at the door. There was a thunderous knocking.

Pete got up, walked to the door and picked up the shotgun. Jake unbarred and opened it.

A man stood outside, tall, dusty, unshaven. He stepped in. Jake moved behind him and shut the door. Pete said, "Hold still until Jake gets your gun."

Jake slid the stranger's gun out of its holster. Pete asked, "Who are you and what do you want?"

"Matt Caine." The man's voice was hoarse and deep. "You got my brother here. I want to see him." He put a hand in his shirt pocket and withdrew a crumpled sheet of paper. He handed it to Pete, who glanced down at it. He recognized the telegraph message he had sent at Caine's request.

He shrugged slightly. "All right. Come on."

Caine stared at him. "What happened to you?"

Pete turned his head. His eyes were cold and his voice was harsh. "The people of this town don't like what your brother did. They went to string him up."

"Been convicted already has he?"

"Not yet. But he will be."

"Don't count on it."

Pete opened the door leading to the cells. He said, "Help yourself." He brought one of the lamps and handed it to Caine. He closed the door.

He sat down on the couch again. He could hear voices behind the door, but could not distinguish words. Jake said, "Maybe you'd better put him in there too, for safekeeping. When the town finds out who he is . . ."

Pete didn't answer him. He waited, and after about ten minutes Caine came through the door, carrying the lamp. He put it down on the desk and looked at Jake. "I'll take my gun."

Jake tossed it to him and he caught it deftly. He slid it into the holster at his side. "He says he didn't do it."

Pete asked cynically, "What did you expect him to say?"

"He'd tell me if he'd done it."

Pete laughed harshly. "Sure. Sure he would."

"What kind of evidence you got?"

"We'll present it at the trial."

Caine walked to the door. He turned and stared hard at Pete. His face was ugly with anger. "I'm just going to say it once, deputy. Turn him loose. Turn him loose now and the two of us will be fifty miles from here in the morning. If you don't . . ."

Pete's eyes were like ice. He said softly, "The girl he attacked is going to marry me. Nobody's going to turn him loose and if you threaten me again you'll be back there in the cell next to him."

Caine unbarred the door and opened it. Standing in the opening he said, "We're a big family, deputy. I ain't the only brother Luke's got. There's four others and they're on their way here as fast as they can come."

Pete said coldly, "Is that supposed to scare me, Caine?"

"It should, deputy. It should." Caine backed out and closed the door. Pete slid the bar into place. He turned and looked at Jake, an odd, uneasy feeling crawling along his spine.

Chapter 11

Pete went over and sat down wearily on the office couch. Caine began yelling back in his cell, but Pete ignored him. He scowled, trying to forget the insistent pain from the beating he'd taken earlier tonight. He had never felt quite as weary as he did right now.

Weariness has a way of obscuring all but the most important things. Right now all he could think was that he meant to hold Caine for trial — against the town — against Matt Caine and the other four brothers he had said would be arriving soon. Beyond that he refused to think of anything.

Jake put his feet up on the desk and closed his eyes. Pete asked, "How long do you suppose it would take the judge to get here if I sent him a telegraph message tonight?"

"Try it and see."

Pete said, "Bar the door behind me when I go out."

Jake's chair creaked as he got up. He grunted assent.

106

Pete put on his hat and went out. He heard the bar slide into place behind him. He fished tobacco out of his shirt pocket, surprised to find it still there. The papers were crumpled but he straightened one out and rolled himself a smoke. He lighted it and drew the smoke appreciatively into his lungs. Then he walked slowly down Butte toward the telegraph office at its lower end.

He liked the way Jake had behaved tonight. He supposed Jake had needed something like this to snap him out of the self-condemning trap he'd been in so long. Maybe it wouldn't be permanent, but it was good to see Jake acting sure of himself again.

There was a light in the telegraph office. The clock on the wall over the telegrapher's desk said eleven-twenty. Pete went in, glad he had thought about wiring Judge Donahue before the office closed at twelve.

The telegrapher, Sam Sikes, turned his head. He wore gold-rimmed spectacles and a green eyeshade. He had black sleeve protectors on his arms, secured by elastic around his upper arms. The instrument was silent.

Pete picked up a sheet of paper and a pencil. He wrote Judge Donahue's name and address on it, then penciled below: "Holding rape suspect for trial. Situation explosive. How soon can you arrive?" He signed his name.

He gave it to Sikes. "Send it right away. I'll wait for his reply."

He walked to the window and stared out while

107

he listened to the clicking of the telegraph key behind him. The sounds stopped and shortly thereafter the instrument clicked out an acknowledgment. He made another cigarette, staring up the street in the direction of the jail. It would take a while, he knew. The message had to be delivered to the judge, his reply carried back and sent. It might be an hour or more.

He hoped he'd get through here in time to catch Doc before he went to bed. The broken rib was continuing to give him trouble every time he drew a breath.

Maybe if he went now . . . by the time Doc was through with him, Judge Donahue's answer should be here. He said, "I'll be back in half an hour. If you don't get an answer soon, jog 'em at the other end."

"All right, Pete." Sikes shoved the eyeshade up. "Looked like things were kind of rough up there a while ago."

"They were."

"How'd you get rid of 'em?"

Pete shrugged. "How do you ever get rid of a bunch like that? Maybe we convinced 'em somebody was going to get hurt if they kept on trying to get in the jail."

"Think Caine did it?"

"He's likelier than Hellman. It was one of the two, that's sure."

He went out and walked up the street. Someone yelled derisively at him as he passed the Butte Saloon. He didn't look around. At Doc's corner he turned and was grateful to see that a light was still burning. He knocked and after several moments the door opened. Doc was in his nightshirt, as he had been the night Julie was attacked. He said, "Come on in, Pete. I didn't figure I'd get much sleep tonight. I'll get dressed and get my bag."

"It's just me, Doc. I think I've got a broken rib. If you could tape it up . . ."

Doc turned his head. "God Almighty, they worked you over good, didn't they? Come on, sit down. Take off your shirt."

Pete unbuttoned his shirt and shrugged out of it. His upper body was a mass of red splotches and bruises now turning from red to blue. Doc probed his ribs with sure fingers. He said, "One's broken all right. What were they doing, kicking you?"

"Uh huh."

"How'd you get away?"

"I didn't. I passed out."

Doc felt expertly of his neck and back, grunting softly to himself as he did. When he had finished he said, "You're damned lucky. I'll tape up that rib."

He got some rolls of wide cloth tape out of the cabinet and began to wrap it tightly around Pete's chest. He kept wrapping until there were several thicknesses. Pete discovered that he could breathe fairly deeply without pain. Doc finished and handed him his shirt. "Try to avoid violent exercise. Let me check those bandages tomorrow."

"All right. Thanks, Doc."

"That eye'll swell shut unless you put some beef-steak on it."

"I'll get some on the way back to the jail."

Doc nodded. "Good night, Pete."

Pete paused at the door. He said helplessly, "I couldn't see Julie this morning. How is she, Doc?"

"Physically she's all right. She isn't over the shock yet, but I doubt if she'll get over that until Caine's been tried and she's had a chance to forget. Right now nobody will let her forget. Her mother's the worst."

"If you see her. . . tell her . . . oh hell, never mind."

"I'll tell her you're doing the best you can."

Pete nodded. "And tell her nothing's changed."

"All right, Pete."

Pete went out, drawing the door closed behind him. He walked over to Butte and along it to the hotel. He went in, through the dining room and into the kitchen, catching Leon and Sally blowing out lamps preparatory to going home. He got a small piece of beefsteak from Leon and went back outside. He was going to need both eyes in the next few days.

He walked down Butte past the two saloons, which were still crowded, and on to the telegraph office at the lower end of Butte. He went in. "Hear anything yet?"

"Yeah. It just came in." Sikes handed him a paper.

Pete read it. It said: "Coming immediately.

Court will convene day after tomorrow at 10:00 A.M." It was signed, "Donahue."

He shoved the paper into his pocket. "Thanks, Sam." He went out. Behind him, Sam hung up his eyeshade and blew out the lamp. He came out, meticulously locking the door and trying it afterward.

He walked up the street beside Pete for about a block, then turned off toward his house. Pete went on alone.

He stopped in front of the jail, enjoying the coolness of the night air, dreading the stuffiness inside the jail. He reached for tobacco, realized the beefsteak was in the way and irritably tossed it halfway across the street. He rolled the smoke, lighted it, and stood there idly smoking it.

Caine was tough, he thought. His brother Matt was even tougher, or Pete was no judge of men. And there were four to come.

He didn't see, though, how five men could change the mood of the town. He knew they couldn't take the jail as long as he stayed on guard against the possibility.

Yet in spite of his self-assurances, uneasiness touched him whenever he thought of them.

The street was fairly quiet now. Many of the townsmen had gone home and what noise there was came muffled from inside the two saloons.

He heard hoofbeats on the hard-packed street and glanced toward the source of the sounds.

For several moments he couldn't see anything, but he could hear the hoofbeats coming closer.

They approached at a walk, from the sounds apparently belonging to several horses.

He frowned lightly. Then he saw three horses pass the Buffalo Saloon, illuminated by the light streaming into the street from the windows and open doors. A moment later they passed the Butte, to be similarly illuminated.

This close, he recognized one of them as Matt Caine. He guessed the others were two of the brothers Caine had said he expected to arrive.

The uneasiness in Pete increased and angered him. Why the hell should he be worried about Caine's brothers? Maybe they were tough, but so was the jail and so was the town. The trial had been set for day after tomorrow at ten.

They pulled up abreast immediately in front of the jail. Matt Caine's voice came harshly from the darkness. "That you, deputy?"

"It's me."

"Want you to meet two of my brothers. Mark and Johnny."

One of the men moved as though to dismount. Pete said sharply, "Stay where you are! Don't get down!"

The figure settled back into his saddle. Matt's voice said, "Edgy, deputy?"

"Maybe."

"You should be. We're here to see that Luke don't hang."

"Your privilege, I guess. To try."

"We'll do more than try." One of the horses detached itself from the others and took several steps closer to Pete. Matt stared down at him, visible now in the small amount of light coming from the windows of the jail. He said softly, "I'll give you one more chance, deputy. Go in and unlock Luke's cell. Bring him out. We'll get him out of town and you'll never see any of us again."

Pete's fists clenched at his sides. His jaw hardened. He'd been pressured about as much as he could stand, by the townspeople, by Julie's mother, by Luke Caine and by Matt. His temper was getting edgier all the time. He said, "Get out of here, Caine. Get out while you can. Don't threaten me again."

"I haven't threatened you yet. I just gave you an out." Caine's voice hardened and turned cold. "Now I'll tell you what the alternative is. Convict Luke or let the townspeople have him and you'll wish you'd never been born. We'll burn this damned hick town to the ground. We'll leave it looking like a battlefield. We'll — "

Pete's anger suddenly got out of hand. He moved like light, slammed against the side of Caine's horse, reached up and seized the man with both his hands. He yanked Caine from his saddle, released him and let him slam against the ground. He stepped in and with deadly precision kicked Caine's hastily drawn gun from his hand.

His own gun was cocked, ready, and his voice was like a whip. "Don't either of you move or I'll kill him like a rabid dog!"

The two brothers froze. Pete said, "Now, one at a time. Drop your guns."

He heard one clatter to the ground, a second moments later. He said, "On your horse, Matt. If I see you on the street before daylight, I'll throw you in with Luke."

Matt grumbled something Pete didn't hear. He jabbed his revolver muzzle into Matt's belly so hard the man grunted sharply with pain. "What was that?"

"Nothin'. Nothin' that won't keep."

"Get going. You can pick up your guns tomorrow."

Matt swung to his saddle. From the horse's back he started to say something but Pete stopped him with a harsh "Shut up! Get out of here!"

Matt's horse moved out and the others fell into line behind. Pete grinned humorlessly to himself as they moved away and disappeared into the darkness. He'd taken some of the arrogance out of them anyway. Not that it would do much good. They'd be back tomorrow. The other two would arrive and then the five would do, or try to do, what they'd come here for.

Pete was determined not to let the townspeople have Luke Caine without a trial, but he was equally determined not to let Luke's brothers take him and get away. If Luke was guilty of attacking Julie, if a judge and jury said he was guilty, then he was going to hang. Pete himself would see to that.

He turned to re-enter the jail. The door was open and Jake stood framed in it. Jake said, "I'm going home. You don't need me any more. Besides, Stone will be back as soon as he's sure nothing's going to happen."

Pete nodded. "All right, Jake. And thanks."

Jake grunted and walked up Butte toward home. Pete picked up the three guns and went inside.

Chapter 12

In summer the dawn came early to the western plains. It began with the faintest lightening of the velvet black of the sky. It grew, turning that inky color to deep gray that faded to a lighter gray. Clouds appeared, and as the sun crept toward the horizon in the east, its searching shafts of light stained those clouds faint shades of pink, tinged with purple that gradually changed to orange and gold.

The top of Gray Butte caught the first visible rays of the sun and it always reflected a cheerful, bright orange color upon the stirring town.

This morning, as the sun touched the uppermost crag of Gray Butte, Matt Caine and his brothers rode down Butte Street and beyond to the edges of the town. Here they halted, dismounted and lounged at the side of the road, smoking, drinking occasionally from a bottle Johnny had and staring across the empty plain along the disappearing road.

In Matt there was no lack of certainty, but there

was anger and there was disgust. Johnny nipped the bottle, offered it to him and was refused. He said, "You think Luke done it, Matt?"

"Sure he done it. She ain't the first." He was thinking of a Cheyenne Indian girl that hadn't been as lucky as Julie Duquesne. She'd put up more fight, he guessed, and that always drove Luke wild. The Cheyenne Indian girl was dead.

There had been others that he'd known about and, he supposed, some he hadn't known about. If Luke hadn't been his own flesh and blood . . .

But Luke was his flesh and blood and he was bound to do what was necessary to keep Luke's neck out of the hangman's noose.

Luke, brother or no, was a damned wild dog. He got up, kicked a rock savagely and stared broodingly along the road. He thought he saw dust in the distance, but he could not be sure. He stared at the place several moments more.

Swinging around, he stared broodingly at the town and at the towering gray mass of earth and rock standing at its western edge. He had to have some kind of plan and he'd better come up with one before the five of them rode back into town. Five men, no matter how tough or unscrupulous, couldn't fight a town. At least not one as angry and determined as this one was. The point wasn't to fight them, anyway. It was to get Luke out of jail and clear.

No ideas came to him. He stared at Gray Butte, wondering why the hell people were stupid enough to build a town at the very foot of such a towering mass of rock. Why, in winter, when alternate thaws and freezes loosened those rocks up there . . . some mighty big ones must break off and come crashing down through the streets below. . . .

The idea grew from there and Matt's eyes took on a fierce and savage gleam. He said, "How hard do you reckon it'd be to get up on top of that damn rock?"

Johnny and Mark stared at it. Mark, youngest of the three, said, "You could ride a horse to the top of the slide and climb from there. Looks like there's two or three of them cracks a man could get up. Why?"

"Just wonderin'." Matt was thinking that they wouldn't have to go all the way to the top. Part way up the sheer cliff would be high enough. If they could go to the foot of the cliff with horses . . . they could do it quickly enough to get everything set before the townspeople even knew what they were trying to do.

He continued to stare at the cliff. About a third of the way up there was a shelf, which from here, at least, appeared to be attainable by means of a crack or chimney running to it from the slide below.

There was the spot they had to reach, he decided. Even in darkness it would not be accessible to the people of the town. Two of them up on that shelf with a few cases of dynamite . . .

Grinning to himself, he swung around and stared along the road again. This time the dust was plain, as were the figures of two men riding just ahead of it.

At this distance it was impossible to recognize them. But Matt knew who they were.

Ten minutes passed and then Matt said suddenly, "All right. Mount up." He swung to his horse. Johnny tipped up the bottle and finished it, tossing it afterward against a rock at the side of the road where it shattered noisily.

The other two, who were Linc and Jess, joined them, and the five rode slowly, abreast, back toward town. Jess, tall, gaunt, the oldest of the five, scratched his unshaven cheek, spat tobacco juice at a lizard running across the road in front of him and asked mildly, "What's Luke done now?"

"Raped some girl in town."

Jess clucked disapprovingly, but without any real dismay. "How're we goin' to get 'im off?"

Matt said, "We're going to that mercantile store on the main street and get us a few cases of dynamite. They won't sell it to us so I suppose we'll have to take it. Two of us are goin' up on that bluff with the dynamite, and a third can stay down below it with the horses. The other two will stay in town. The townspeople will do what we tell 'em to or the whole damn bluff is going to come crashing down through their lousy town."

Jess said approvingly, "That'll work! By God, Matt, that'll work!"

Matt drew his horse to a halt in front of Delehanty's Mercantile. He swung to the ground. "Jess, you and Linc stay here. Johnny, you and

Mark come in with me."

He went up the steps, crossed the narrow veranda and entered.

Apparently the store had just been opened. Delehanty, a thickset, elderly man, walked up the long aisle toward them.

Matt said, "I want some dynamite. About five cases, I guess. And fuse and caps."

Delehanty stared at him doubtfully. "Stranger, ain't you?"

"Uh huh."

"Then what do you need dynamite for?"

Matt slid his gun from its holster. He thumbed the hammer back with an audible click. "I want five cases of dynamite and fuse and caps. How much?"

"Won't sell it to you. Not without an okay from Sheriff Stone."

"Then we'll take it. Where's it kept?"

Delehanty's mouth firmed with stubbornness. Caine said softly, "We don't want to hurt you, mister, but we will if we have to."

Delehanty stared closely at Matt's narrowed eyes. Then he shrugged. "All right. It's out in back."

Matt said, "Mark, you stay here."

"All right, Matt."

Matt looked at Delehanty again. "Get the key and let's go."

As they went through the back room, piled high with canned goods and boxes, Matt snatched up half a dozen gunny sacks. Carrying them, he followed Delehanty to a small frame shed behind the store.

He tossed the sacks to Johnny. Delehanty stared at him briefly, then unlocked the door. Matt said, "Carry 'em out here and open them."

Delehanty began to carry cases out. When he had finished, Matt asked, "Fuse and caps in the store?"

"Uh huh."

"All right. Bust these boxes open."

Delehanty took a pinch bar from a nail on the shed door and began to pry open the cases. Matt helped. When they were all open, he dumped them in the sacks, one case to each sack. He kicked the boxes aside. Delehanty relocked the door. Matt said, "You carry two, storekeeper. Johnny, you take a couple. I'll bring the other one."

Delehanty and Johnny each picked up two sacks. Matt brought the other, still holding his gun in his right hand. They went back inside and up front to where Mark waited for them. Matt said, "Mark, you and Johnny carry these out. I'll get the other stuff."

The two went out, carrying the sacks. Matt said, "Get the fuse and caps. Hurry up."

Silently Delehanty led him to the rear of the store. There was a box chest-high on the wall, and it was padlocked too. He opened it, gave Matt a large coil of black fuse and a small box of metal caps. He turned his back to lock the door. Matt raised his gun and brought the barrel slashing down. . . .

Delehanty slumped without a sound. He lay crumpled on the floor at Matt's feet. Matt turned and went outside, after first holstering his gun. He said, "Come on."

He swung to the back of his horse. The five rode up Butte Street toward the upper end of town. Where the street petered out, there was a narrow trail zigzagging across the steep slide to the foot of the sheer rock cliff. They rode up it, single file.

It took less than five minutes to reach the foot of the cliff. Here they dismounted. Matt said, "Linc, get your rifle out. Keep an eye down below until I get back."

He put the coiled fuse into one of the sacks. Then he took his rope from his saddle and, carrying it, began to climb up the fissure in the rock.

It varied from a foot in width to about three feet. In spots the rock was worn smooth, indicating that others had climbed it before. Probably the kids in town, he thought.

It was easy to climb. He reached the shelf in about ten minutes and lowered down one end of his rope. It was a thirty-five-foot rope and it allowed just enough slack so that the lower end could be tied to a sack if a man held the sack as high as he could.

Matt pulled up the first sack, untied it and lowered the rope for the second. In less than ten minutes he had all five sacks on the shelf with him.

He called, "Johnny, you and Mark come up. I'll bring you food and water later on today."

Johnny came first and Mark followed. When they reached the shelf, Matt laid the dynamite sticks as far back in the fissure as he could, after first stuffing in the sacks to make a nest for it. He inserted a length of fuse into one of the caps, crimped it with his teeth, then pushed the cap into one of the sticks of soft, claylike dynamite. He laid this stick back among the others and put a rock on top of it to hold it firmly in place. He led the fuse out and along the shelf, allowing what he judged was a ten-minute length. Johnny and Mark had to have time to get down safely before the charge went off, but it had to be short enough so that no one could get up in time to yank the fuse.

He went back and laid rocks on the fuse where it emerged from the fissure so that it would not accidentally be yanked out. He looked at Johnny. "Got matches?"

Johnny nodded. Matt said, "The signal will be three quick shots, a pause and then two more. If you hear it, light the fuse and get the hell out of here fast. Get out of town. We'll meet at Santa Rosa, forty miles south of here."

"What about horses?"

"I'll leave Linc at the foot of the cliff with three of them."

"All right, Matt."

Matt started down the fissure. "You probably won't get the signal at all. But have matches handy in case you do."

"Sure."

Matt eased himself down the fissure to the top of the slide where the others were. He said, "Linc, you stay here with the horses. If you see anybody leaving town, lay a couple of shots in the ground ahead of 'em. If they don't turn back, cut 'em down."

Linc nodded.

"I'll send you up some food and a bottle."

"Thanks, Matt. Good luck."

Matt nodded at Jess. "Come on, Jess. We got a call to make."

They mounted and slid their mounts down the steep, zigzagging trail to the bottom of the bluff. They rode at a trot down Butte. Matt pulled up in front of the sheriff's office and yelled, "Sheriff! Deputy! Come out here!"

Pete and Stone came to the door. They stepped into the street warily.

Matt pointed at the bluff. "Look up there. Two of Luke's brothers are on that shelf with five cases of dynamite. Linc's down at the foot of the cliff with horses."

Stone's face was an odd shade of gray. He said, "Good God, man, surely you don't intend to . . ."

Matt laughed shortly. "Five cases all going off at once would loosen some sizable chunks of rock, wouldn't they, sheriff? And they'd all come rollin' down through town."

"You wouldn't . . ."

"Wouldn't I?" Matt's eyes were cold. "You know better than that, sheriff."

Pete clenched his jaws. "What do you want?"

"We want Luke. And we want a whole day's start."

"How the hell could we guarantee that? The townspeople . . ."

Matt laughed again, harshly. "With that much dynamite up there, I doubt if anyone's going to argue much." His eyes gleamed suddenly with the birth of a new idea. "Maybe we'll let him go to trial. Maybe he'll be acquitted. When's the judge due to arrive?"

"Tonight or tomorrow morning. Court will convene at ten tomorrow morning."

"Then pass the word around. Let the town know what it's up against. It'd be a shame if I had to signal them up there — just because some damn fool did something rash."

Pete stared up at Caine. He said softly, "You won't get away with it, Caine. Right now I don't know how I'll stop you, but I will."

"You try it, deputy. You try it. But be ready to dodge some rocks when you do. Some damned big rocks."

Chapter 13

Pete watched Matt and his brother Jess ride away. He was scowling savagely, but there was a helpless quality in his eyes. Stone said heavily, "Looks like they got us where the hair's short."

"The hell they have! Caine isn't going free. Not if I have to kill him myself!"

"You had a chance to kill him once."

"I know it." He stared angrily at Stone. His mind was racing, but racing futilely like a squirrel in a cage. There just wasn't any answer. Not to a threat like this. Five cases of dynamite exploding up there would bury the town. It would wreck half the houses and kill most of the people.

Stone said, "I'd better go spread the word."

"They'll run. They'll run like rabbits."

"I doubt if he'll let 'em run." Stone glanced at Pete's face, then turned and walked heavily up the street. At the hotel, Pete saw Caine tacking up some kind of notice on one of the veranda posts. He watched while Caine stepped away and saw several passers-by stop to read it. Immediately their eyes went to the face of the bluff where the two Caine brothers were plainly visible.

They saw the sheriff and hurried to him, chattering excitedly. Stone was plainly trying to calm them down but he wasn't succeeding. Pete turned and went into the sheriff's office. He kicked the door shut savagely.

For ten or fifteen minutes he paced back and forth like a wolf in a cage. His mind darted from one impossible solution to another. In the end it came right back to its starting point. There wasn't any answer. There wasn't any way of defeating Caine and his plan.

The door flung open and Delehanty, the storekeeper, staggered in. There was a streak of dried blood on one side of his face and a place on the top of his head that was matted with it. His eyes were both pain-filled and angry. "Those strangers . . . they made me give them five cases of dynamite. Then they hit me. I just came to. . . ."

"I know, Mr. Delehanty."

"Ain't you going to arrest them? What kind of lawman — ?"

Pete said, "Come here a minute, Mr. Delehanty." He went to the door and opened it. He stepped into the street, with Delehanty doubtfully following. He pointed at Gray Butte. "Two of them are up there on the face of the butte. They've got the dynamite planted in that seam. A third one is down below with the horses."

Delehanty stared in unbelief. "What do they want?"

Pete gestured with his head toward the jail. "They're his brothers. Caine's. They want him out."

"What are you going to do?"

"I don't know. I haven't decided."

Delehanty was staring at the bluff. "Five cases! God!"

"How much rock do you figure those five cases will bring down?"

"Half the butte. No, not that much, but enough to bury the town!"

"And where would it fall?"

"Head of Butte Street."

"That's what I thought." Julie's house was at the head of Butte Street, directly beneath the Caines and their dynamite.

Delehanty took another look at him, then staggered up the street, mumbling, "This is crazy! I'm going to get out of here!"

Pete watched him go, scowling. His fists clenched when he thought of that dynamite blasting loose thousands of tons of rock and all of it falling on Julie's house. Julie and her family were going to have to get out. They couldn't stay.

But, he told himself, there wasn't any immediate danger. Caine wasn't going to risk everything by blasting the rock face loose. Not yet. And the town wasn't likely to provoke him into it.

He should have killed Luke Caine when he had the chance. He admitted it now. Things were completely out of hand and either the town was going to be wrecked or Caine was going to go free.

Stone had disappeared The street was crowded with excited townspeople. A dozen of them came hurrying down the street toward Pete. Among them were Del Pomeroy, Hight and Hughie Smithers, the clerk at the hotel. Pomeroy said breathlessly while he was still a dozen feet away, "Pete, you've got to turn him loose. They'll kill half the people in town if you don't."

Pete shook his head. "I'm not going to turn him loose. He's going to trial."

"They'll — "

"No they won't. As long as Caine's in jail the town is safe enough. This is pressure to keep us from hanging him."

"I say let's turn him loose. We don't even know — "

Pete stared angrily at them. "Last night you wanted to hang him. You wanted to take him out of jail and string him up. Have you changed your minds about his guilt or do you lose your principles when you get scared?"

Pomeroy flushed and so did several of the others. Then Pomeroy's glance raised and met Pete's. "Rub it in if you want. But one man ain't important when a whole town's in danger."

Pete glanced up Butte Street. Pomeroy's house wasn't very far from Julie's and it was right in the path the avalanche would take. He said stubbornly, "Caine's going to trial. He's guilty and he's going to hang if I have to spring the trap myself!"

129

Pomeroy's face turned gray. He glanced up the street and back again like a rabbit looking for a place to hide. "I'm going to get my family and get out of here!"

He turned, pushed through those behind him and began to run up Butte. The others glanced at Pete's set face, turned and followed him, each heading toward his own home. Along the street people were scattering similarly.

Pete hadn't seen where Stone had gone. He wished the sheriff would come back. He wanted to go up to Julie's house and warn them to get out, but he didn't dare leave his prisoners.

A buggy came careening down Butte, whirled past Pete, raising a cloud of dust, and continued toward the edge of town. Pete glanced up at the butte. The sun glinted on a rifle barrel and he saw a puff of smoke.

He glanced at the buggy again in time to see the horse go down. The buggy flipped sideways, landed on its side and skidded crazily. Occupants spilled from it, a man and a woman. The woman got up and stumbled toward her husband, who lay quite still.

Pete hesitated a moment. With a good rifle . . . The range from here to the man at the foot of the butte was about three hundred yards. He could get him and maybe the two on the shelf, but not before they lighted the fuse. The range was too long for any certainty.

He turned and ran toward the overturned buggy. One yellow wheel was still spinning crazily. The horse was thrashing in the shafts, but he did not get up.

The woman, Delia Bronson, was kneeling beside her unconscious husband. She was not crying. There was blood on her face, and dust, and her clothes were torn.

Pete knelt on the other side of Ed Bronson. He could see the man's regular breathing. He looked closely at his head. There was a bleeding gash on one side of it just over the ear.

He said, "He's all right, Mrs. Bronson. Just knocked out. I'll get someone to help you take him home. Then you stay there, understand?"

"Aren't you going to do something? Those men — "

"Those men aren't going to do anything as long as this town sits tight. They want their brother and I've got him in jail."

"Then give him to them."

He said, "Mrs. Bronson, your husband was one of a bunch that almost beat me to death last night. They wanted Caine and they wanted to hang him. Now you want me to turn him loose."

She looked confused. Pete got to his feet. He asked a couple in the gathering crowd of men to help her get Ed home. Then he walked around to where the horse lay and put a bullet in his head.

A man came down the street, riding a galloping horse. Pete yelled at him to stop, but he thundered on past. The rifle up on the butte opened up with a thunderous racket, each shot magnified by the bluff face itself. Dust puffs kicked up all around the running horse. The man hauled up, glanced at the bluff, then turned and rode the horse slowly back toward Pete. As he went past he mumbled, "I'll wait for night. By God they can't shoot me in the dark."

Pete returned to his office. The town was thoroughly frightened and confused by now. They were realizing they couldn't leave, not without taking a chance on getting shot.

They also realized that they didn't dare stay. Not with Pete flatly refusing to compromise.

Stone came around the jail from the rear. He glanced at the frightened people in the street. He looked sheepishly at Pete. Pete asked, "Where did you go?"

"Home. I was going to get my wife out of town but . . ."

"Going to stay here for a while?"

Panic briefly touched the sheriff's eyes. Pete said, "I'm not going to run away. I want to go up to Julie's. I want them to get out of there. They haven't got a chance if the dynamite goes off."

"All right. I'll stay here." Relief was evident in the sheriff's voice.

Pete walked slowly up the street, occasionally glancing up at the men on the face of the bluff. Temptation was strong to round up half a dozen men with rifles and get as close as possible and then cut them down. But it was too big a chance, he realized. The closest anyone could get was two hundred yards and all that the men up there would

132

have to do to escape being shot was throw themselves flat on the shelf. They could light the fuse and no one could stop them.

Tonight . . . He wondered if he could get up that slide trail and surprise the man with the horses at the foot of the cliff. He supposed it was possible. He also supposed it was possible to climb the fissure and overcome the two on the shelf. But the odds against achieving it successfully were a hundred to one. He'd have to think of something else.

He saw Matt Caine ride up the trail at the head of the street carrying a gunny sack and two canteens. He dismounted at the foot of the cliff. A rope was lowered from the shelf and the sack and one canteen hoisted up.

Caine mounted again and came riding down. He met Pete in front of Julie's house. He grinned mockingly. "Ready to come to terms, deputy?"

"Not yet. As long as Luke's in jail, you won't set off that charge. If you do, you know Luke's going to get a load of buckshot in his guts."

Matt's grin didn't waver, but his eyes hardened. "I'll figure some way to get you before we leave."

"If you leave."

Matt didn't reply. He stared at Pete coldly for a moment and then rode deliberately down the street.

Pete went to the door of Julie's house and knocked. Mrs. Duquesne came to the door, flushed and angry, but Pete stopped her before she could speak. He said brutally, "You keep still. I've heard all I want to hear from you. I came

133

to tell you that you'd better get out of this house. There are two men up on the bluff right above here with five cases of dynamite. They're threatening to explode it unless I turn Caine loose."

The color faded from her face. She turned and screeched, "Jules! Julie! Come here, quick!"

Julie and her father came running down the stairs. Pete stared hungrily at Julie's face as he repeated what he had told Mrs. Duquesne. That awful blankness seemed to be gone from her eyes but she wouldn't meet his glance. Duquesne said, "We'll leave. We'll go to the Taylors."

Pete nodded shortly. He said, "Caine isn't going to get away. No matter what happens, he isn't going to get away."

Chapter 14

Pete waited at the gate for ten minutes, watching the house, hoping that Julie would come out first and that he would get a chance to talk to her. But when she appeared, it was in the company of both her father and mother. He watched them walk toward the Taylor house on the south edge of town, each carrying a small bag.

Reluctantly he headed back down Butte Street toward the sheriff's office. Once, he turned and stared up at the face of the butte.

The pair on the shelf were sitting there indolently, their backs to the stone face of the butte. They were smoking and their hats were tilted over their eyes against the morning sun.

Down below where the horses were, the third man leaned on his rifle, watching the town.

The streets were strangely empty and silent now. Those who had planned to leave had been discouraged by the experience of the Bronsons. Pete could see the overturned buggy and the dead horse still lying in the middle of Butte Street beyond the sheriff's office.

He reached the place. Stone was sitting on the bench in front, puffing on his pipe. Pete sat down and fished in his pocket for makings. He rolled a smoke and lighted it before he asked, "Where is everybody?"

"They're havin' a meeting in the lobby of the hotel."

"To decide what?"

"How to make us turn the prisoner loose."

"And if we won't?"

"Then they're going to try and get out of town as soon as it gets dark."

"Caine won't let 'em."

"I don't know how the hell he's going to stop them."

"He'll think of something. You can count on that." He was silent for a moment and then he said, "Shouldn't the sheriff's office be represented at the meeting?"

"I suppose it should. Why don't you go?"

Pete got up. He didn't particularly want to go because he knew the abuse that would be heaped on him. But he admitted that he should. He walked up the street to the hotel and entered the lobby.

There were about seventy-five people there, mostly men. Pete saw Delehanty, his head wrapped with white bandages. Doc Bonner was there. So were Del Pomeroy, Lex Massey and Frank Hight. Bronson and his wife were present, he also bandaged and looking sick. As Pete entered, Pomeroy shouted, "Let's all stop talking at once and see if we can't decide something!" He saw Pete and yelled, "There's Chaney. What are you going to do, Pete? Turn him loose?"

Pete shook his head. Someone yelled, "What the hell has he got to say about it anyway? Stone's the sheriff and Chaney is only his deputy. He'll do what Stone tells him to."

Pete stared at the speaker, recognizing Jack Call, one of those who had participated in the attack on him last night. He shouted, "The judge is due sometime tonight. Trial starts at ten in the morning. Caine will be there."

"Supposing Stone turns him loose?"

"Stone isn't going to turn him loose." Pete's eyes were angry and hard. "Nobody's going to turn him loose. Not as long as I'm alive."

"That might not be too long."

Pete shoved his way through the crowd to Call. He backhanded him across the face. "Are you threatening me? How'd you like to share Caine's cell?"

Pomeroy caught Pete's arm. "Stop it, Pete. This isn't getting us anywhere."

Pete swung his head, thoroughly angered now. He said, "Isn't it?" He raised his voice. "When I brought Caine in, every damn one of you criticized me because I didn't bring him in dead. Twice you tried to take him out of the jail so you could hang him. There isn't a one of you that's any more law-abiding than the Caines. But whether you like it or not, Caine's going to have an orderly trial. What you do with him at the trial is your business, I guess. You'll either turn him loose or convict him. But you're going to have to do it in a courtroom. I'll no more turn him loose without a trial than I'll give him to you to lynch."

Call said sullenly, "Then we're getting out of town. Tonight, as soon as it's dark. You won't have a jury to try him with."

Pete stared contemptuously at the crowd. "I doubt if I'd have that anyway. I doubt if there's twelve men in town with guts enough to serve on it."

He turned and stalked out of the hotel. Matt Caine and his brother were standing on the veranda, listening. Matt's face was twisted into a triumphant grin. He gestured with a toss of his head at a notice he had just finished tacking to one of the veranda posts. It was crudely lettered with charcoal. It read, "Notice. If anyone tries to leave town, night or day, I will signal my brothers to explode the dynamite." It was signed, "Matt Caine."

Caine said, "You'd just as well give up, deputy. Turn him loose. He probably didn't do it anyway. It was probably the one you've got in jail with him."

Pete said, "Your brother ran. Hellman didn't. Figure it out for yourself."

"So what if he did do it? The girl's alive, isn't she?"

Pete's action was wholly reflexive. His fist swung, burying itself in Caine's belly. As Caine doubled, he brought up a knee that connected squarely with Caine's nose. It spurted blood like a fountain as he sprawled forward at Pete's feet.

Pete's gun was in his hand before Caine struck the floor. He yelled, "Don't!" and Jess Caine's hand froze touching the grips of his holstered gun. Pete felt cheated. He wanted a chance to fight it out with Caine. He wanted an outlet for the frustrated fury boiling in him. But he didn't dare holster his gun or Jess would shoot him. And he couldn't fight Matt with a gun in his hand.

The man came to hands and knees, shaking his head. Blood dripped steadily from his nose to the veranda floor. Those inside the hotel lobby came boiling out, to surround Pete and Jess and Matt, who was just getting up. Del Pomeroy yelled, "Look at this!" He read the posted notice loudly.

Matt shoved his way through the crowd to Pomeroy. He said harshly, "If it wasn't for Luke, I'd signal 'em right now. I'd like to see that bluff come rollin' down through this stinkin' town!"

Pomeroy edged his way to where Pete stood. "You didn't have to do that! You'd better watch out or you'll crowd them too far. And then where will we be?"

Pete turned disgustedly and tramped downstreet toward the sheriff's office. Behind him the voices of the crowd rose excitedly. He realized he was sick to death of that crowd. They were a bunch of sheep, first wanting this, then wanting that. What he ought to do . . .

He considered the prospect with grim pleasure. What he ought to do was get Julie and ride away from Gray Butte. Let them figure the way out for themselves. Only doing that would mean Caine's freedom.

But wouldn't he go free anyway? What jury picked from the terrified people of this town would convict him as long as the Caines and their dynamite remained on the face of the bluff?

Stone was still sitting on the bench in front of the jail. The door was open and Pete could hear Luke Caine yelling for something. He pulled the door shut so he wouldn't have to listen.

Stone coughed, then said, "Guess you think I ran out last night."

"Didn't you?"

"Well, maybe I did." Stone's voice was both defiant and resentful. "I figured that mob was going to take you and Jake apart."

"Why didn't you come out and help?"

Stone's face flushed with anger. "Don't you talk to me in that tone of voice! You're only a deputy and I can fire you any time I want."

Pete said coldly, "Go ahead. Fire me."

"Don't push me or I will. I just made up my mind last night that Caine wasn't worth killin' people for. Or worth gettin' killed either, for that matter. And he isn't."

Pete said, "With a man like Caine, you can be damn sure Julie isn't the first. And she won't be the last, if he gets loose."

"We could turn him loose and then get up a posse and go after the six of them."

Pete said, "Yeah. You could do that. And all

140

the Caines would have to do would be to split up. You couldn't split your posse six ways. You might get a couple of 'em. Then you'd be back where you are right now."

He glanced up Butte and saw a determined-looking delegation heading toward the jail from the hotel. He also saw something else that brought him instantly to his feet — Julie Duquesne, alone, turning the corner onto Butte a block away.

He moved out swiftly. He brushed past the delegation, ignoring their efforts to stop him, saying only, "See Stone. He's the sheriff."

He went on, almost running, his glance resting anxiously on Julie's face.

He reached her and stopped. For an instant they stood facing each other, saying nothing.

Her face was pale, her eyes enormous. Her lips were almost colorless and the lower one was trembling.

Pete took her arm and turned her around. He walked her to the corner and turned it with her. He walked in silence until they reached the edge of town. Then he asked worriedly, "How do you feel?"

She tried to smile, but it wasn't a successful smile. He headed downhill through the weeds until he reached the shade of a cottonwood. He said, "Sit down, Julie. I tried to see you but your mother . . ."

"I know, Pete. I heard."

He said almost humbly, "Maybe I didn't do right, but I did what I thought was right."

"I know it, Pete. That's why I came — to tell you that. I didn't mean it before when I told you I wanted you to kill him."

He said, "Nothing's been changed, Julie. I wanted to see you and tell you that. When it's over we're going to get married and go away from here."

"Will it ever be over, Pete?"

"Sure it will. Caine's going to trial tomorrow."

"But they'll turn him loose. They don't dare convict him with those men and all that dynamite up there on the bluff."

Pete said firmly, "They won't turn him loose. Between now and then maybe I can . . ." He stopped, realizing how impossible it was to change the odds. He couldn't reach the men on the bluff before they could light the fuse. There was no use fooling himself.

He stared at Julie's face, remembering the laughing light that had been in her eyes before. He couldn't help thinking of Caine manhandling her and when he thought of that, fury tore like a holocaust through his mind. He didn't know what was going to happen tomorrow. He didn't know if they'd be able to get a jury that would try Caine impartially. He had to admit the possibility that Caine would be acquitted.

If he was . . . He clenched his jaws knowing that more than anything else in the world he would want to pursue and kill Caine himself. But would he? Could he kill Caine and thus set himself above the law, above judge and jury who had tried him and set him free? Were his principles so shallow that he would violate them the first time the law didn't do exactly as he thought it should?

Julie said, "I ought to go back. Mother will worry. . . ."

"All right." He lifted her to her feet. Suddenly she was clasped tight in his arms and her body was shaking with sobs.

She cried, "Pete, how can we get married? I'll never be the same. Every time . . . every time you touch me I'll think of him! I won't want to but I won't be able to help myself!"

"That's not so, Julie. This has happened to other girls, and it hasn't spoiled their lives." He tilted her face up and kissed her lightly on the mouth. "You can't let it spoil yours. You need time, that's all. Time to forget."

"Yes, Pete." She pulled away and dried her eyes. He knew she didn't believe. But she would. She had to. Eventually, when the horror of all that had happened dimmed . . .

He walked her back toward town, unable to avoid staring up at the face of the bluff. Julie said softly, "They'll really do it, won't they?"

"I'm afraid they will."

"Can't you take him over to Santa Rosa for trial?"

Pete nodded. The same thing had occurred to him. He said, "We'd never get him there unless we could get up a posse big enough to fight off the Caines. And they'd stop anyone from joining the posse by threatening to explode the dynamite."

"They can't stay up there forever."

"No, they can't. The thing is, they don't want to explode the dynamite any more than we want 'em to. They know if they bury this town with rock that they'll all eventually be hunted down. But they do want Luke and they'll bury the town if they have to to get him."

They had reached the outskirts of the town. Julie said, "Don't come home with me, Pete. You know how bitter Mother is."

He grinned. "I know. When will I see you again?"

"Tomorrow, I guess, at the trial. I have to testify, don't I?"

He nodded. "Think you're up to it?"

"I don't know. I'll try."

He took her hands and squeezed them. Then he watched her walk away toward the Taylor house where she and her parents were staying. He headed toward the sheriff's office again.

Right now this whole mess rested squarely on his shoulders and he didn't know how he was going to get it off.

Chapter 15

The delegation of townspeople, which he had passed going to Julie, was still at the sheriff's office when he returned. No mob this time but an orderly, scared group bent not on violence but on avoiding it. He went into the open door. "What's going on?"

Del Pomeroy seemed to be spokesman. He said, "We're trying to work this out."

Pete said harshly, "You're not trying to work it out. You're trying to get Caine turned loose."

"What if we are? Is that so terrible? If that dynamite goes off, even if it doesn't kill anybody, it will wreck thousands of dollars worth of property."

Pete said, "Nothing doing."

"Who the hell do you think you are anyway? You're Stone's deputy, not sheriff. You don't have a damn thing to say about it." This was Rufus More, the blacksmith, who had shouldered his way to the front of the group.

He was a huge, thickset man in overalls and

long underwear but no shirt. The neck of his underwear was open, revealing a thick, hairy chest. He looked at Stone. "How about it, Stone? You can fire him any time you want, can't you?"

Stone said, "I can, but I'm not going to. Pete went out and brought Caine in. He's a good deputy. He hasn't done anything to get fired for. All he's trying to do is enforce the law and that's what he's paid to do. Besides, Julie and him are engaged to be married. Next to Julie, he's the one that's been hurt the most."

"Next to Julie?" The blacksmith snorted. "How do we know it was rape? How the hell do you know Julie didn't make eyes at him and then try to back out when the going got too rough?"

For the barest instant Pete was too stunned to move. He heard the words, but for a split second they did not penetrate his consciousness. When they did — he flung himself at More, face twisted, eyes blazing ferociously.

More outweighed him by thirty pounds. He was thick with muscle. His chest had nearly twice the girth of Pete's and below it his stomach bulged beneath his overalls. His legs seemed spindly by comparison with his upper body but that was a deceptive thing. They were strong and quick as well.

Pete's fist smashed his nose and Pete's momentum bowled him back into the crowd. Several of them went down. The others scrambled toward the door.

Stone yelled, "Pete!" but he might as well have

saved his breath. Pete didn't hear and if he had he wouldn't have stopped. He buried his fist to the wrist in the blacksmith's belly and drove a huge, sour grunt of air from the man's mouth. He followed with a left to More's mouth that split his lips like ripe tomatoes.

Until now, the blacksmith had been as surprised as Pete. Now his tiny eyes blazed with a ferocity equal to Pete's own. He crouched like a wrestler, both arms extended, both hands open.

Pete knew what More wanted. He wanted him close, so that he could crush him in those powerful arms.

The office was clear now, except for Stone. Pete rushed again, striking More with the point of his shoulder. The man was big, and hitting him was like hitting a wall, in that only surface damage seemed to result. Pete's fists felt as though they were broken.

His shoulder drove another gust of air from More and the force of his whole body's weight drove the man back against the gunrack with a crash. The guns clattered to the floor. More rushed him and Pete side-stepped at the last instant, letting him go plunging past. More hit the sheriff's desk, moving it two feet in spite of its weight and size. The sheriff's swivel chair toppled backward, spilling Stone to the floor. When More turned, there was a slightly dazed look in his tiny blue eyes.

Never in his life had Pete been more enraged. He wanted to kill the blacksmith in the same ferocious way he had wanted to kill Julie's attacker on the night of the attack. Because More's attack was, in its way, as bad as the original attack had been. Caine had attacked her physically but More was attacking her reputation, her decency, and that was even worse.

And not because he honestly believed it, either. He was scared, that the Caines might blast loose their rock upon the town, that his house and his blacksmith shop, both standing directly in the path of that avalanche, might be destroyed.

Pete rushed again, his eyes narrowed, his mouth the merest slit through which teeth showed in an almost animal snarl. This time he brought up a knee, and followed with an elbow to More's thick throat. The man gagged and choked, but he had Pete in his arms and kept him there as though they were a vise.

Pete's knee came up again, savagely, and the excruciating pain made the arms loosen momentarily. Then they clamped down even harder than before.

More whirled, holding Pete's feet clear of the floor. Pete kicked frantically against his shins. He might as well have been kicking a tree for all the good it did.

Those crushing arms . . . He felt his chest constrict until breathing was restricted to short, shallow gasps. Pain from the broken rib, which had virtually disappeared when Doc taped his chest, returned, worse than ever before. His head began to spin.

More turned toward the desk. He laid Pete's back on its sharp edge and bore down hard.

The pain that shot through Pete's body was the worst he had ever known. He twisted frantically but without success. His arms, pinned at his sides, were useless. His feet, though they were free to kick, seemed unable to hurt More badly enough to make him loosen his hold. More meant to break his spine, Pete realized, and then drop him, helpless and forever crippled, to the floor.

His hand touched the grips of his gun. He yanked it out. He couldn't raise it, so he thumbed back the hammer and fired it from where it was.

More's grip loosened, and Pete doubled his legs, bringing up both knees for leverage. Straightening them, he broke free of More's hold, skidded across the desk and fell in a pile on Stone's overturned chair.

He tried to get up and failed. He put his hands on the chair and used it for leverage to force himself to his feet. He still held his gun in his right hand.

There was blood soaking through the left leg of More's pants from a wound that appeared to be just above the knee. The man was staring down at it as though he couldn't believe it. He lifted his head and stared at Pete.

Then he turned and lunged toward the pile of guns that had spilled from the rack to the floor. Stooping, he seized a double-barreled ten-gauge and swung it around.

Most of the guns were kept loaded and while

it was possible this one was not, Pete couldn't afford to take the chance. Hanging onto the overturned swivel chair, he raised his revolver and thumbed the hammer back.

His voice didn't sound like his own as he croaked, "Drop it, More. Drop it or I'll shoot."

More hesitated, the shotgun half raised. There was recklessness in the blacksmith's eyes and Pete knew it was a fifty-fifty chance that he would elect to shoot.

Support came from an unexpected quarter. Stone's voice cut through the silence like a knife. "You heard him, More. Drop it or you'll get it from him and me both!"

The starch went out of the burly blacksmith. He eased the hammers down and let the gun clatter to the floor. Pete said, "Now get out of here. You're getting blood all over the goddamn floor."

More stared down at his drenched pants leg. Limping, he went to the door. He turned there, to stare balefully at Pete. He seemed about to speak but Pete stopped him with a harsh, "Your big mouth has already gotten you into enough trouble. Don't let it get you into any more."

More whirled and went into the street. Pete holstered his gun. He went over and dazedly righted the sheriff's swivel chair. He sank into it.

Stone crossed the office and began to replace the guns in the rack. Neither man spoke. Gradually Pete's breathing became easier, and he said, "Thanks for backing me up."

Stone turned. He asked, "What the hell are we

going to do? What *can* we do?"

Pete said, "We've only got two choices. We let Caine go or we hold him and bring him to trial."

"What good will that do? With Caine's two brothers on that shelf with dynamite . . ."

"Maybe something will happen."

"What *could* happen? They've got us exactly where they want us and you know it."

Pete said irritably, "How do I know what could happen? I know something could, that's all. I don't see any reason for giving up yet."

"What's the use of bringing Caine to trial? There ain't twelve men in this whole damn town that would find him guilty now."

"If we can't get a jury here we'll take him to Santa Rosa."

Stone laughed sourly. "Who'll take him? I won't. Not with five of them Caines determined to keep us from getting there."

"Then I'll take him. And he won't get away. I'd put a bullet in him before I'd let them take him away from me."

"They'd kill you."

Pete shrugged. "They figure on doing that anyway before they leave."

"I wish to God we'd never sent that telegraph message to Caine's brother in the first place."

"We couldn't know there were five of 'em."

"Well, at least the townspeople have given up the idea of lynching."

"Yeah." Pete had never felt more tired than he did right now. The past few days had been filled with strain. The two beatings he'd taken hadn't helped.

He wondered if it would ever be over or if it would go on and on forever like this. That was silly, of course. But it seemed like six months since Julie had come running hysterically down the hill, a blanket covering her nakedness. . . .

Thinking of that made him angry again, made him more determined than ever that Caine should pay for his crime. If there was just some way he could remove the Caines' threat to the town. . . .

He considered capturing the Caines, Matt and Jess, and holding them as hostages. If he threatened to kill them unless the brothers came down off the rock shelf above the town. . . .

He said, "What if we were to arrest Matt and Jess for robbing Delehanty's store? What if we held 'em here and told the two up on the shelf that we'd kill 'em unless they came down . . . ?"

He knew the answer even before Stone shook his head. Taking Matt and Jess was too risky. He didn't know what the signal was and Matt might possibly succeed in giving it before he was subdued. He didn't dare risk the lives of the townspeople that way. Fifty people might be killed if that avalanche of rock came down. . . .

Besides, neither he nor Stone could carry out such a threat even if they did succeed in subduing Matt and Jess. They couldn't cold-bloodedly murder the pair and the Caine brothers up on the bluff would know they couldn't.

Then how about calling Matt Caine's bluff? How

about going ahead and convicting Luke and hanging him? They could keep watch on the two up on the shelf. If they started to leave . . .

It would take them at least ten or fifteen minutes to get clear of the blast themselves. The townspeople would have that much time to evacuate the town.

Again he reluctantly shook his head. The Caines could get clear faster than the townspeople could. Some of the townspeople were sure to be left behind and caught. . . .

Pete cursed softly to himself. It was an impasse, out of which there seemed to be no way except the release of Luke. But he wasn't going to release Luke yet. He would stall as long as he possibly could.

Chapter 16

At sundown there was an air about the town — of terror so tangible you could feel it in the nearly deserted streets. Those who walked the streets did so silently, their heads down except for an occasional fearful glance at the two on the bluff.

As gray dusk crept across the land, a tiny fire winked on the shelf above the town, reminder that the Caine brothers were still there, reminder of the threat they constituted.

The stage rolled into town at eight and drew to a halt in front of the hotel. A single passenger alighted, to be met by Pete Chaney as he stepped from the coach.

Pete took the man's hand and said, "Hello, Judge Donahue. I'm glad you could come tonight."

Donahue was a tall, gaunt man in his seventies. He wore a small gray goatee and a rather magnificent cavalry-style mustache. He was dressed in a severe black suit, a white shirt and black tie. He took his carpetbag from the driver when it was handed down and turned toward the hotel. In the light filtering from the hotel windows, he studied Pete's face. "Is something wrong?"

Pete grinned ruefully. "Everything's wrong, Judge."

"Come on upstairs and fill me in."

"Sure." Pete walked with him to the desk where the judge registered and got a key. He followed Donahue upstairs and into his room. He lighted the lamp, then closed the door. Donahue said, "Now. What's going on here?"

"Well, when I wired you the people were trying to get the prisoner out of jail and lynch him."

"I don't see any crowds now. What happened?"

"We held the jail all right. Maybe we couldn't have kept on holding it, but then the prisoner's five brothers arrived. They held up Delehanty and took five cases of dynamite. They hauled it up to that shelf on the bluff face and there they sit, threatening to set it off unless we turn the prisoner loose."

"But you haven't turned him loose?"

"No. And I won't."

"Why?"

"Why should I? They don't dare set off the dynamite any more than the town dares convict and hang Caine. It's a standoff."

"Who was the girl?"

"Julie."

"Julie Duquesne? Good God!" The judge studied Pete's face more closely. "You and she were going to be married soon, weren't you?"

"We still are. As soon as this stinking mess is cleared up."

"What have you got on the prisoner? What kind of evidence?"

"There were only two strangers in town the night it happened, and Julie said it was someone she didn't know. One of them ran and one stayed. I went after the one that ran and he resisted arrest."

"That isn't much."

"I know it. But he had scratches all over his face. And I figure Julie can identify him."

"Was it dark?"

"Yeah. It happened in the old Satterlee house."

"Then how can she identify him?"

"I figure she can."

"You've got more than that, haven't you?"

Until now, Pete hadn't realized how weak was his case against Caine. He said, "That's all I've got."

"Then you'd better turn him loose because it isn't enough. I'd have to instruct the jury . . ."

Pete said suddenly, "You sit tight, Judge. I'll get more. Before tomorrow morning at ten."

"I hope you know what you're doing."

"I think I do."

"Then I'll see you tomorrow at ten."

"All right, Judge." Pete went out. There was only one kind of evidence he could get against Caine now. He had to have a confession, an admission of guilt.

Under ordinary circumstances, he realized,

Caine would never confess. But these were not ordinary circumstances. Caine knew his brothers were up on the bluff with dynamite. He knew the townspeople were pressuring the sheriff and his deputy to turn him loose. He must know, that, regardless of evidence, they wouldn't convict him tomorrow.

About now Caine would be cocky and insolent. He could probably be taunted enough . . .

He went downstairs and through the lobby. Even if he got a conviction tomorrow, he thought, even if Judge Donahue instructed a reluctant jury to bring in a verdict of guilty, it wasn't going to do him any good. The Caines were still up on the bluff.

He wasn't going to think about that. He was going to go ahead and get what he needed to convict Caine. He'd told Stone that something might happen, and maybe it would. Maybe the situation would change.

Hurrying, he went up Butte and turned the corner at Jake's street. He strode swiftly to Jake's house and outlined the plan he had in mind. He needed witnesses to Caine's confession if he was able to get it. Stone and himself and Jake and Hellman would be four. Four would be enough.

Jake walked rapidly beside him, puffing a little with shortness of breath. Once he said, "They've changed their tune since the Caines climbed up on the bluff, Pete."

"Yeah. They sure have." He was frowning to himself, trying to think of a way he could taunt

Caine into a confession. They reached the sheriff's office and went inside. Pete said, "The judge is here."

Stone shrugged. He was sitting at his desk with his feet on it.

Pete said, "I'm going to talk to Caine."

"Go ahead."

Pete picked up a lamp. He went to the door leading to the cells and opened it. He left it ajar about six inches.

Hellman was sitting on the side of his bunk, his head in his hands. Caine was lying down, and he did not get up. He looked mockingly at Pete. "What now, deputy? I'm practically a free man."

"You're not free yet."

"Why don't you face it, deputy? You're licked. You can't let my brothers blast that rock down into town."

Pete said, "I'll have your brothers in that cell with you before I'm through."

"For what?"

"Armed robbery. Aggravated assault. Attempted murder."

"What the hell are you talking about?"

"They didn't buy that dynamite. They took it at the point of a gun. They slugged the store-keeper and they tried to kill Ed Bronson and his wife."

Caine grinned lazily. "Matt's a heller, ain't he?"

"He's a man, and that's more than I can say for you. I'm even beginning to doubt if you're the one we want. Hellman back there would be a likelier choice."

"Why?"

"Because he's got more guts than you. You're yellow, Caine. You're yellow clear through. I doubt if you've even got guts enough to attack a girl."

The grin left Caine's face. "When I get out of here, I'll show you how much guts I've got."

Pete snorted contemptuously.

Caine's eyes suddenly gleamed. He licked his lips and began to grin again. "Maybe I won't kill you after all, deputy. Maybe I'll just take your girl with me when I go."

"You dirty bastard . . . !" Pete took hold of the bars with both hands. His knuckles turned white. He was sick at his stomach and suddenly didn't want to hear any more. But he stayed, and glared helplessly at Caine.

Caine chuckled. "Yeah. Maybe I'll do that. Maybe I'll take her with me. She might not fight so hard next time . . ." He stopped, sobered by the look in Pete's eyes. Then he got to his feet and shouted, "You talk about guts! You ain't got the guts to touch me, even when I stand here and tell you I raped your girl. Because if you do touch me your whole damn town is going to get buried!"

Pete kept his grip on the bars, knowing if he let loose he'd draw his gun and kill this man. He heard movement behind him and turned his head. Jake stood behind him and, with a swift, sure movement, Jake slipped Pete's gun from its holster. He said, "Now you can let go of those bars. You got what you wanted. Stone and me heard it. So did Hellman, didn't you, Hellman?"

"Yeah. I heard it."

Caine shouted, "So what? I'm not goin' to trial. I'm ridin' out with my brothers tomorrow."

Pete said softly, "You're going to dangle on the end of a rope." He understood why Caine had admitted attacking Julie. He had taunted Caine enough to make the man's hatred leap out of control. Caine had wanted to hurt Pete, for the capture, for the contempt Pete had heaped on him. . . . And once he'd started talking the confession had just slipped out. . . .

Pete turned suddenly and strode outside. He went through the sheriff's office and out into the night. There had never been any real doubt in his mind that Caine was guilty. But hearing the man taunt him with it . . .

He was almost to the edge of town before he realized where he was or realized that he was practically running. He stopped and gulped the cool night air into his lungs.

With hands that shook, he withdrew tobacco and papers from his pocket and rolled a smoke. He lighted it, puffed almost frantically until it was gone. He threw it down and stepped on it.

And he knew something he had not known before. He couldn't let Caine go. If somehow they forced him to, it wouldn't be the end of it. It couldn't. He'd track Caine down and kill him. He'd do that no matter how long it took.

Caine had hurt him all right back there. But he had also doomed himself, no matter what Stone or the townspeople did. No matter how the trial came out.

Morning was clear and cool. Sunlight struck the top of Gray Butte early and crept downward toward the sleeping town as the sun rose higher and higher above the eastern plain.

Up on the shelf, smoke rose from a small fire as the pair up there made coffee and cooked breakfast for themselves. The town stirred, and the streets held a scattering of people, nervous, frightened people who glanced often and with open fear at the face of the bluff.

There was no courthouse in town, but there was a large, empty room over Delehanty's Mercantile Store that was used for trials. The county rented it from Delehanty for ten dollars a month.

Pete got a cup of coffee at the hotel, then climbed the outside stairs and unlocked the courtroom door. It had been more than a year since any trials had been held here and the place was dusty.

He got a broom and swept. Then he began to place the folding chairs in rows facing the small raised platform at one end. He was glad of something to do. It was just after six, which left almost four hours until time for the trial to begin.

It took him almost an hour to clean the place and arrange the chairs. When he had finished he opened the windows that faced the street to let the dust he had raised clear out.

After that he went, somewhat reluctantly, back down the stairs. He got two trays in the hotel kitchen and, carrying them, returned to the jail.

There was, fortunately, no indecision in him any more. He knew precisely what he intended to do. He would take Caine to the courtroom at ten o'clock and he would testify against him just as he would against anyone accused of a crime. It was up to the town and the judge to either convict him or set him free.

But if they set him free . . . No longer was Pete hampered by conscience with respect to Luke Caine. Caine had admitted attacking Julie. He was guilty and he was going to die, whether it was by the rope or by Pete's gun. Caine didn't know it, but he had doomed himself last night. Five brothers — fifty brothers wouldn't keep him from Pete's vengeance now.

Stone was up. He was standing before the cracked mirror on one wall of the jail, his face lathered, shaving. He turned his head as Pete came in. "Morning." He shaved one cheek carefully, then said, "Hadn't we better turn Hellman loose? We know he's clean."

"Let's hang onto him until after the trial. He's a material witness now and I don't want him to get away."

"Guess you're right." Stone finished and toweled his face. He carried the pan of water out in back and threw it on the ground. He returned and sat down at the desk to eat.

Pete wasn't hungry, but he forced himself to

eat. He felt like choking every time he thought of Caine gloating back there in his cell.

He was just finishing when the door opened. Matt and Jess Caine came in.

Matt's face held a triumphant expression. He said, "Ready to turn him loose, sheriff? Or do we have to go through the whole rigmarole of a trial?"

Stone said, "We'll have the trial."

Matt grinned. "Maybe that's better anyway. Maybe it's better to have him cleared before we take him and get out of here."

Pete didn't speak. Matt glanced at him, still grinning. "You're quiet this morning, deputy. Finally admitted you're beat?"

Pete said, "I'm not beat. Now get out of here."

"We came to see Luke. We got a right . . ."

Pete got up. He could feel his temper slipping. "I said get out of here. You're not going to see him. You have no rights at all. You're both guilty of crimes in Gray Butte."

"Ain't going to arrest us, are you, deputy?"

Pete said softly, "Go on. Or you may have to follow through on your threat and neither of us wants that, do we?"

Caine scowled but he said, "Come on, Jess," turned and stepped out the door. Jess followed him silently.

Chapter 17

By nine o'clock people were beginning to gather for the trial. Both saloons filled and spilled their crowds over into the street. Up in front of Delehanty's Mercantile, a knot of people had gathered. They stood, mostly silent, dividing their attention between the two men on the face of the butte and the jail farther down the street.

Pete paced back and forth inside the sheriff's office. Stone sat at his desk, his feet on it, puffing his pipe and occasionally repacking and relighting it.

He showed no emotion but, Pete thought, that didn't mean he was feeling none. His impassiveness explained the reason he had been able to hold down the sheriff's job so long without anyone realizing he wasn't up to coping with serious trouble if it came.

Pete wondered if he would break, and when. It would be sometime today, probably, at the time of greatest danger. He had run out on his job once and there was no reason to believe he wouldn't run out on it again.

At nine-thirty Pete went into the back part of the jail, two sets of handcuffs dangling from his hand. He went to Hellman's cell first, unlocked it and put the cuffs on Hellman's outstretched wrists. He said, "All right. Go on up front."

Hellman disappeared through the door leading to the office. Pete heard Stone's swivel chair creak as he got up.

He unlocked Caine's cell. "Come on."

Caine crossed the cell to him. Pete said, "Turn around and hold your hands out behind you."

Caine started to say something, took a look at Pete's face and changed his mind. Obediently, he turned around and extended his hands behind him. Pete put on the cuffs, snapping them tightly around Caine's wrists.

His jaws were clenched with his effort to maintain his self-control, but he managed it and said curtly, "All right. Get going."

Caine walked into the office. Stone handed Pete a shotgun and a handful of shells. Pete broke the gun and loaded it. He put the rest of the shells into his pocket.

Abruptly he changed his mind. He handed the shotgun back to Stone and crossed to the gunrack. He took down a rifle, checked to see if it was loaded, then got more shells for it from the drawer.

Caine said, "If you're thinking about picking off my brothers up on the butte, don't. You'll — "

Pete said, "Shut up." He gestured toward the

165

outside door with the rifle barrel and Caine went out. Hellman followed and Pete came out immediately afterward. Stone brought up the rear.

Hellman and Caine walked abreast up the walk toward Delehanty's store. Stone and Pete walked immediately behind. The least of Pete's worries was that Caine might escape but he was watchful anyway.

They reached the store and Pete said, "Upstairs."

The crowd broke and made way. There were people ahead of them on the stairs, and these people hurried as though not wanting the two prisoners to get too close to them.

The courtroom was about half filled. The judge had not yet arrived, so Pete took his prisoners to chairs in the front row. He seated himself immediately behind them. Stone went back to the door to wait for the judge.

Voices inside the courtroom were hushed, but in the aggregate they made a noticeable hum. The minutes dragged endlessly past.

Pete realized that his hands were sweating. He wiped them, one by one, on the legs of his pants. Hellman sat hunched down in his chair, staring straight ahead. Caine sat up straight, watching the door for his brothers.

They came in about ten minutes before ten, Matt and Jess, and crossed to where Luke sat. Matt stared at Pete for a moment, then at his brother Luke. "We'll have you out of this before night, Luke. Sit tight."

Stone had left the door to follow the Caines, and now he said softly, "Move along, you."

Matt swung his head and looked at the sheriff. He said, "Come on, Jess," and the pair moved on to the end of the row of seats, where they sat down. Both wore expressions of amused contempt.

The judge came in shortly after they had seated themselves. Stone said, "Stand up, everybody."

The people got to their feet. Donahue crossed to the desk at the front of the room and sat down. He rapped on the desk with the battered wooden gavel he had brought with him.

The crowd quieted. Donahue looked at Stone. "We'll select a jury first. Will you call up about fifteen men?"

Stone began to call off names. As he did, the men called rose to their feet and moved to a double row of chairs at the left side of the judge's desk. Stone called up fifteen.

Pete studied their faces, one by one. They wore, without exception, expressions of reluctance, even of sullen defiance. When the courtroom had quieted again, Donahue said, "Call them one by one, sheriff." He turned his head toward the prospective jurymen. "As your name is called, please rise and face the bench."

Stone said, "Pomeroy."

Pomeroy got up. He glanced uneasily at the prisoner, then at Matt and Jess Caine. He didn't look at Pete.

Judge Donahue said, "Are you a qualified elector of this county?"

"Yes, sir."

"Is there any reason why you cannot sit on a jury in the case pending before this court and render a fair and impartial verdict according to the evidence presented?"

Pomeroy looked at the floor. "I reckon there is, Judge."

"What is the reason?"

"I reckon I've already made up my mind. I reckon the evidence wouldn't change it much."

Donahue studied Pomeroy for a long time. Pomeroy met his gaze defiantly but with uneasiness. At last Donahue said, "Excused. Call the next man, sheriff."

"Frank Hight."

Hight stood up. Pete already knew what he was going to say. He'd gotten his cue from Pomeroy. He also knew that, no matter how many days they sat here calling prospective jurors from among the people of the town, they weren't going to get twelve, or even half that many, who would be willing to serve.

And perhaps it was just as well. The way things stood in Gray Butte now, a jury would acquit Caine anyway. And once acquitted, he would be forever free.

Hight gave the judge the same answer Pomeroy had. Stone called another, and another, and another.

As the farce went on, Judge Donahue's face darkened. When the fifteen had all been excused, he faced the crowd. For several moments he was silent. Then he said, "In all the years I have served on the bench it has never been my misfortune to encounter such a depraved and cowardly town. A crime has been committed here, as vile a crime as men commit, against a girl liked and respected by all of you!"

He glared at the subdued crowd, not one of which would meet his eyes. "You are allowing yourselves to be intimidated. You are thereby condoning the crime."

He sighed heavily. "Nor is that the worst of it. Until the defendant's brothers showed up and threatened the town, you tried several times to force the jail and take the law into your own hands. I wish I could indict the lot of you — both for interfering with the sheriff in the performance of his duties, and for being accessories to the crime that has been committed here. Unfortunately I cannot. There are too many of you. But I can tell you how contemptible you are. And I can warn you . . . if you try to crucify the girl against whom the crime was committed to ease your own dirty consciences, I'll personally see to it that everyone uttering a word against her will be called to account."

Judge Donahue glared at the crowd contemptuously. Then he said, "I therefore instruct the sheriff and his deputy to conduct the prisoner to Santa Rosa immediately. Trial will convene there tomorrow at ten o'clock. Perhaps in Santa Rosa there are twelve men with courage enough to sit in judgment on the defendant in this case. Court adjourned."

He got up. Stone rose too and said harshly, "Stand up."

Spectators and the defendant rose. The judge walked to the door and disappeared.

Pete dug his rifle into Luke Caine's back. He looked straight at Matt. "I'm just going to say this once. Try interfering and I'll pull the trigger. You may get me, but that won't save Luke. Stay where you are until we're out the door."

Stone faced the crowd. "All of you stay until the prisoner is outside."

Pete prodded Caine with the muzzle of the rifle. Caine grunted with pain, but he moved toward the door. Pete said, "Slowly. Don't give me any reason to think you're trying to duck away from the muzzle of this gun."

Caine glanced over his shoulder at Pete's face. He moved out toward the door, slowly and deliberately. He stepped onto the landing and started down the steps.

Pete stayed a step behind, the muzzle of the rifle prodding Luke from behind. He heard steps on the landing behind him, but he did not look around.

They reached the street level. Pete said, "Hold it a minute."

Caine stopped and Pete glanced quickly around. Stone was standing on the landing, the shotgun pointed back into the courtroom. Hellman was with him but no one else was visible. He swung his head and said, "Take a look."

Caine turned his head. After that he walked ahead of Pete almost dejectedly all the way to the jail.

Pete took off his manacles and locked him in, seeing doubt in Caine's eyes for the first time. Caine whined, "I'm out of tobacco and matches. Hell it looks like — "

Pete said, "Later." He returned to the office and after several moments Stone came in with Hellman. Stone unlocked Hellman's manacles. "You can go if you want to, Hellman. Only stay in town until we're ready to leave for Santa Rosa."

"Can't I ride over there alone?"

Stone shook his head.

"Then I'd as soon stay in jail. I ain't got a cent."

"Suit yourself." Stone followed the man back to his cell and locked him in. He returned to the office.

Pete asked, "When do you want to leave? We'd better go right away or we'll have to travel at night."

"Are you crazy? We'd never get Caine there. We'd never get him out of town."

"We've got to try. I'll go get the horses. Be back in twenty minutes."

Stone didn't reply. Pete went out and walked down Butte to the livery barn. He went in and yelled for Cass Bruhn. The man stuck his head out of one of the stalls. Pete said, "I want four horses, Cass. Right away."

"You taking him to Santa Rosa now?"

Pete nodded.

"By yourselves?"

"Our job, I guess. If the townspeople wouldn't serve on the jury I doubt if they'll help us now."

"You'll never make it."

Pete didn't answer that. He said, "The horses, Cass. Hurry it up."

Cass began to lead the horses out and after that to saddle them. Pete watched, knowing that Cass had spoken the truth. He and Stone wouldn't get Caine to Santa Rosa. They didn't have a chance.

But Caine wasn't going free and he wasn't going to escape. He was going to do one of two things: stand trial in Santa Rosa, or die by Pete's own gun.

Cass finished saddling the horses. Pete gathered up the reins of three of them and swung astride the fourth. He rode into the street.

Up in front of the hotel a crowd had gathered to read something Caine had tacked up on one of the veranda posts. Pete rode up the street, past the sheriff's office to the hotel. He rode through the crowd until he could read Caine's crudely lettered sign. It said, "My brothers will stay on the bluff. If anyone but the sheriff and his deputy leave town with the prisoners they will light the fuse."

Caine stood beside the sign staring up at him mockingly. Pete stared back. Caine would let them get five or ten miles from town. Then he'd pull his brothers off the bluff and they all would come after Luke. Stone and Pete wouldn't stand a chance against five like the Caines.

He shrugged inwardly and turned back toward the jail. He reached it, swung down and looped the horses' reins around the rail. He went inside.

He froze as he stepped inside the door. Caine was standing there, his hands free. Stone was heading back toward the cells in the rear. His back was turned.

As Pete entered, Caine lunged toward the gunrack over against the wall. Pete yanked his revolver, thumbed back the hammer and said sharply, "Hold it!"

Caine froze. Pete said loudly, "Stone? God damn it, did you expect him to stand here and wait for you? Come put the handcuffs on him!"

Stone turned. There was a gun in his hand. He said, "Let him go, Pete."

"No!" Pete stared at Stone in unbelief. The man was full of contradictions. He had backed Pete a while ago over Delehanty's store. He had backed him earlier in the fight with More. Now he was selling out. . . .

"Let him go," Stone said heavily. "I won't tell you again."

"Then shoot. But I'll get Caine before you can knock me off my feet."

"Pete. . . ." There was an almost frantic tone in the sheriff's voice. "This is best. Believe me, this is best."

Pete said, "Put the gun away and bring me the handcuffs."

Stone came into the office. He flung the handcuffs at Pete's feet. He put a hand to his shirt and tore the star from it. He flung the star across the room. "To hell with it! I'm through. Any time I haven't got more sense than to throw my life away on a dirty bum like this . . ."

He looked once more at Pete. Then he stepped out the door. He turned downstreet and went out of sight.

Chapter 18

Pete stared after him for several moments, trying to keep the dismay he was feeling from showing in his face. Then he swung his head. He said, "Caine, I'm alone now and I'm edgy. Don't do anything sudden and don't give me any grief. Turn around."

Caine turned around.

"Put your hands out behind you."

Caine obeyed.

Pete stooped and picked up the manacles. He snapped them, one by one, on Caine's wrists. He hesitated a moment, then said, "Back in your cell."

Caine moved out, through the door and into his cell. Pete closed and locked the door.

He returned to the office and slammed the connecting door. He walked to the window and stared broodingly into the sunwashed, dusty street. He had no idea what he was going to do now. He hadn't a chance of making it to Santa Rosa alone. And he knew no one would help.

Right now he needed time to think. Not that thinking would change anything. But there ought to be some way. There had to be!

He sat down gloomily in the sheriff's chair. He rolled a smoke with fingers that trembled slightly, lighted it and puffed deeply. He reviewed his actions since the night Julie had come running, hysterical and hurt, down the hill to him.

Now, he guessed he should have killed Luke Caine. It would have saved a lot of trouble all around. Yet if he had, he would never have heard Luke's confession of guilt. He would never have known for sure. . . .

And yet, knowing for sure, acting strictly according to his principles since the night of the attack — these things were now going to cost him his life.

It never occurred to him to quit, as Stone had. But he was scared . . . in a way that put ice in the middle of his stomach. He didn't want to die. Most of all he didn't want to sit here and contemplate it like a man condemned to die for a crime.

He shrugged fatalistically. There was no way of saving his own life. But if he stayed alert every step of the way at least he could get Caine before they got him.

He got wearily to his feet. No use stalling or putting it off. It was a thing that must be done and there was no use delaying it.

He thought of calling on Jake, then shook his head. Asking Jake to help would be asking for

Jake's life too. And this wasn't Jake's job. Not any more.

It was almost noon and if he didn't start soon it would be dark before he arrived. His mouth twisted wryly. He wasn't going to arrive, so what did it matter? And yet, there was that slim, hairline chance. . . .

He went into the rear of the jail and unlocked Hellman's cell. He said, "I don't want to risk your neck, Hellman. If I let you go alone will you promise to go straight to Santa Rosa and wait for me?"

Relief was plain in Hellman's face. He nodded. "I'll be there, Mr. Chaney."

Pete fished ten dollars from his pocket. "For a room and meals. No whiskey, understand?"

"Sure, Mr. Chaney. Thanks."

Pete said, "Take one of the horses that are tied out front. But hang around town until the Caines come down off the bluff. They might shoot at you if you don't."

"Yes, sir." Hellman went out and stood for several moments on the walk, blinking in the bright sunlight. Then he unwound the reins of one of the horses from the rail and swung to the saddle. He rode away downstreet.

Pete walked heavily toward the cells in the rear. He wished he could see Julie before he went, but he couldn't. He didn't dare leave the jail unguarded, and there wasn't a soul who would watch it while he was gone.

He heard the office door open behind him and swung around warily. Julie stood in the doorway,

177

looking at him timidly.

He slammed the connecting door leading to the cells and went to her. She glanced around the office, then asked, "Where's Mr. Stone?"

"He's not here right now." No use worrying her unnecessarily. No use telling her that Stone had gone and would not be back.

"Are you going to take Caine to Santa Rosa?"

"Yes, Julie." He put his hands gently on her shoulders. He told himself to be careful not to say anything that might let her know how deadly things really were.

She said, "Mother and Father and I will leave early tomorrow morning. We'll be there by ten."

He nodded, his eyes devouring her face. Most of the shock was gone from her, he realized suddenly. He said softly, "I love you, Julie."

Her arms went up and around his neck. She stood on tiptoe for his kiss.

It was long and sweet and in spite of his weariness, his hurts and the despair that was like lead in his mind, it stirred old fires.

Breathless, she drew away. "I wanted you to know, Pete. . . . Before you go, I wanted you to know that I think you did exactly right in everything."

He grinned at her. "Thanks, Julie. I'd rather hear that from you than from anyone else."

"I've got to go now. I'll see you tomorrow."

"Yes, Julie. Tomorrow."

She went out and he stepped to the window and watched her until she disappeared. The old carefree swing had returned, partially at least, to her walk.

His expression sobered. He went back to the cells and unlocked Caine's door. "Come on. We're going. And I'm just going to warn you once. Try to escape — make any wrong move at all and I'll kill you. I haven't got much chance of reaching Santa Rosa, but then you haven't either. If your brothers get me, I'm going to get you before I fall."

Caine was sobered by his words. The mocking light, the contempt, were gone from his eyes. He said, "Make a deal with them. They don't want to kill you and neither do I."

Pete grinned sourly at him. "Changed your tune, haven't you?"

Caine nodded. There was unconcealed fear in his eyes.

In the office, Pete halted him. He got Stone's double-barreled ten-gauge from the rack. He broke it and checked the loads to make sure they were buckshot. He withdrew a couple of extra shells from the drawer though he knew he'd never have time to reload. He said, "With both barrels, I can't miss you, Caine. Remember it. If I shoot, I'll cut you in two."

Caine seemed unable to take his eyes from the gun. He licked his lips, swallowed and said, "Deputy . . . they're going to try. They'll try to kill you and get me away."

"I know they will. But if I don't kill you, you'll hang. So what do you care? One's no easier than

179

the other." Pete couldn't help the bitter pleasure he felt at Caine's terror. "Go on out and mount up."

Caine shuffled out the door. He stood beside one of the horses while Pete unlocked one of the handcuffs and relocked it with his hands in front of him. He swung up and Pete handed him the reins.

He untied one of the other horses and mounted. He glanced up Butte.

It was lined with people, almost to the end of it, as though in expectation of a parade. Silent people. People whose faces were all turned this way.

Pete said, "Move along. Down toward the lower end of town."

Caine touched heels to his horse's sides. Pete held the double-barrel cradled in his arms. He rode on Caine's right and slightly to the rear so that the gun muzzle bore on his prisoner every second of the time, however carelessly it appeared to be held. They'd have to hit him in the head to stop him from firing the shotgun and there wasn't much chance of that.

Caine swung his head and stared up at the butte. He said, "They're still up there."

"They'll come down when we're clear of the town."

"There's only two. Linc's gone from the foot of the cliff."

Pete quickly swung his head. He saw two horses tied at the foot of the cliff, but nothing else. He ran his glance along Butte Street, looking for Matt and Jess and Linc, but he didn't see any of them. He turned his head and stared down Butte Street, paying particular attention to the building tops. He saw nothing there either.

Would they try it before he cleared the town, he wondered. And if he killed Luke, would they explode the charge on the cliff anyway, just for revenge?

No use worrying, he thought. No use thinking. He knew what he was up against and neither thinking nor worrying would change a thing.

Half a block now lay between them and the jail. Pete realized he was holding his breath. Waiting.

Almost a block now. He released his held breath in a long, slow sigh, but did not relax the thumb that was hooked over one of the hammers of the gun.

The shot cracked out so unexpectedly that he flinched. The hammer of the shotgun came back. . . .

Caine halted his horse. Pete halted too, wondering why he was not hit, wondering who had fired that unexpected shot.

Then the echo reached him, reverberating back from the face of the butte. Immediately he understood. That shot had not been fired by either of the two on the butte. It had been fired by someone here in town.

Not the Caines, either. If they had fired it, Pete would have been hit. He frowned with puzzlement. He moved his horse half a dozen yards ahead so that he could keep his eyes on Luke when he turned.

Turning, he glanced up at the face of the butte in time to see one of the Caines catapult from the shelf. A long, thin wail reached his ears, the involuntary cry of the falling man.

Shocked, he remained motionless, helplessly watching as the second man up there knelt to light the fuse.

Again the unseen rifle spoke, and again, after several seconds, the echo of the report reverberated back. But the second man was hit. . . .

The man stood up, staggered to the wall of the butte and leaned against it. The rifle spoke a third time and the man was slammed against the rock face of the butte. He slumped and sat down, head hanging limply to one side. He did not move again.

For several seconds Pete was motionless, stunned. He had become so used to the threat up on the cliff that it was hard for his mind to accept the fact that it was gone.

When he did realize, the jail was more than a block away. Somewhere, unseen, were the three Caine brothers who yet remained alive. . . .

He faced a choice: ride out of town, stop where he had cover and hold them off until help arrived from town, or return to the jail.

Either course was dangerous. He stared at Luke, then up Butte Street. His thoughts screamed, "Move! Do anything but do it quick!"

Sight of the confusion and panic in the street decided him. The townspeople who had lined the street were dispersing like frightened quail. They were running, scattering. . . .

They believed the fuse had been lit. They were trying to get clear of town before the dynamite went off.

Maybe the fuse had been lighted by the second man up there before he was hit. But whether it had or not, it would be some time before Pete could expect any help from the people of the town. . . . For an hour or more they would be concerned only with escape and, if the dynamite failed to go off, with returning to their homes.

The squat jail looked to Pete as though it was a thousand miles away. He shifted the shotgun slightly in his hands. He said, "Back to jail, Caine. And you'd better be praying that nothing happens between here and there."

Chapter 19

Caine swung his head and stared at Pete. There was open terror in Caine's eyes now. Two of his brothers were dead and the shock of that, of seeing them die, was plain in his eyes. Pete thought sourly that he'd probably thought the Caine tribe was immortal and couldn't die. He knew better now.

He said, "Move, damn you! Move!"

A stunned Luke Caine touched his horse's sides with his heels. The pair moved slowly toward the jail.

Pete didn't shift the shotgun but kept it pointed straight at Luke. There was a kind of buzz in the air, the sound of many voices shouting throughout the town. Pete wondered briefly who the unseen rifleman had been. Jake, he supposed. It could have been no one else. Only Jake would have guts enough to take such a chance with the safety of the town. Only Jake had enough contempt for it to risk it so recklessly.

How many minutes had passed since Jake's rifle killed the second man up on the bluff? It seemed like an hour, but Pete knew it could have been no more than a minute or two at most.

Half a block remained. Ahead of him, Caine's head jerked back and forth as he scanned the building tops and second-story windows between him and the jail. His face was almost gray with fear; his eyes were wide with it.

Good, Pete thought. Perhaps Caine was now feeling some of the same kind of terror his brutal attack had inspired in Julie several nights before.

One thing Pete knew — if the Caines, the three of them, stepped out to block his way, he hadn't a chance of reaching the jail. No one man can cope with four.

He might get help from Jake but he couldn't count on it. Jake might be several blocks away. He would have wanted to be as close as possible to the butte when he picked off the Caines up there. . . .

Caine rode past the Butte Saloon. Pete heard the doors as he passed. He turned his head and saw Matt come into the street, immediately followed by Jess and Linc.

Then he was past, keeping pace with Luke so that the range would not lengthen too much for effective use of the scattergun. Behind him Matt's harsh voice called, "Hold it, deputy!"

Pete said, "Pull up, Luke."

Luke's horse stopped. Pete sat motionless, without turning, his finger tense against the trigger of the ten-gauge. The muzzle pointed straight at Luke.

Impasse again. But an impasse where Pete was at a disadvantage. For all he knew, Matt might be taking careful aim at his head right now.

He said, "Drop your gun, Matt. Tell your brothers to do the same. The shotgun's trained on Luke and my finger's tight against the trigger. Even if you was to hit me in the head, it would go off. You going to take that chance?"

"What chance? Luke's dead anyway if you get him to that jail."

The compulsion to turn his head was overpoweringly strong in Pete. He resisted it stubbornly.

Behind him, the shot blasted with complete unexpectedness. As it did, Luke dug heels into his startled horse's flanks and reined violently aside.

Stunned briefly by the realization that no bullet had touched him, Pete held his fire for the split part of a second. Then his finger tightened down. . . .

Only the edge of the shot pattern struck Luke and his horse. Luke flinched and flung himself forward over his horse's withers. The horse, superficially wounded, pounded up Butte at a fast, hard run.

Too late, Pete realized that the shot behind him had been a feint, fired either into the air or into the ground. It had been meant to precipitate things and bring them to a head.

He flung himself off his horse, reigning violently right as he did so that the animal would be between him and the Caines. He heard two guns fired almost simultaneously and heard one of the bullets strike his horse.

He was running, trying to keep his balance and turn in time. . . . He overran the horse, which stumbled and collapsed into the dust. He whirled, thumbing back the hammer of the second barrel.

A third shot blasted, this one fired by Linc, and was followed almost instantaneously by a fourth and fifth, from Matt and Jess.

Something like a mule's kick struck Pete in the thigh. Then the deep boom of the shotgun momentarily wiped out all other sound.

At a range of less than twenty feet the buckshot pattern went almost altogether into Linc, standing closest of the three to the doors of the saloon. It tore into his face and chest, bringing an instant rush of blood that drenched his shirt and spurted in rivulets from his face.

The force of the blast drove him back as though he had been struck by the rush of air from a terrific explosion. He slammed into the saloon window, which was shattering from the buckshot that had missed him and gone past, in time to fall and be showered with fragments of falling glass. And Pete was left with an empty gun, at the mercy of the remaining two. . . .

Whether they failed to realize that his shotgun held only two loads, whether their stunned minds failed to grasp the fact that he had fired both, he never knew. They had only to stand, calmly and dispassionately, and shoot him down. Yet they chose to run.

Jess dived back into the saloon. Matt, farther

from the door, ran upstreet and ducked between the saloon and the building next to it.

Pete wasn't thinking now. He was acting on instinct. He broke the shotgun and punched the two extras into it. He lunged toward the doors of the saloon as he snapped it shut.

He burst through the doors, nearly falling as his leg gave beneath him. He could feel the warmth of blood all the way to his ankle, and his pants leg was stuck to it with blood.

Jess ducked behind the bar. Pete swung the gun muzzle toward him, holding fire at the last instant as Jess disappeared.

Those who had been in the saloon poured frantically out the doors and into the street, nearly trampling each other in their anxiety to escape. Pete plunged across the room toward the end of the bar where Jess had disappeared.

His leg was numb and treacherous. He rounded the end of the bar just as Jess stood up and fired.

Pete thumbed back the right-hand hammer. He fired instantly.

Again the devastation was terrible. The charge cleaned the back bar as thoroughly as a cyclone might have cleaned it, shattering every bottle, shattering the mirror too.

It practically cut Jess Caine in two. His abdomen a mass of blood and gore, he doubled like a jackknife and went down, to be covered by liquor and falling glass.

Pete whirled and ran stumblingly to the doors. He burst into the street. His eyes were wild and his hat was gone. He stared to right and left, looking for Matt.

Several of the men in the street pointed at the passageway beside the saloon. Pete lunged into it. He didn't know how much longer his leg would hold up. He still wasn't thinking straight. He only knew he had to get Matt before he collapsed from loss of blood.

The passageway was empty ahead of him. He stumbled along it, reached the end and ran into the clear.

A pile of trash unexpectedly barred his way. He stumbled and fell headlong. . . .

From ahead and to the right a gun spat viciously. The bullet thudded into the saloon wall behind Pete.

He rolled as the gun spat at him again. He kept thinking, "One load. One load is all I've got." He had completely forgotten his holstered revolver and it was as well that he had. It was gone, lost in front of the saloon when he flung himself from his horse.

He saw Matt as he rolled, saw him standing behind a sagging, graying fence. Only Matt's head and chest were visible. And his hand, holding the gun that unerringly followed Pete's motion as he rolled.

Pete stopped his roll and fought to bring the shotgun to bear. He was looking straight into the muzzle of Matt Caine's gun, seeing the gray end of one bullet and several empty chambers behind it. Beyond that was Matt's face, twisted with a combination of fury and grief.

Pete knew he could not fire in time. He knew that in an instant Matt's gun would belch flame and smoke and the bullet, so carefully aimed, would end his life.

He'd almost made it, though, he thought. Almost. . . .

Matt jerked violently and spun around. His gun, no longer pointed at Pete, discharged. Then the sound of a rifle reached Pete's ears, the same deep boom he had heard before.

Matt disappeared and only the sagging, graying fence remained. Pete glanced around and saw Jake standing with a rifle in his hands on a building top across the alley half a block away.

He got up and staggered to the fence. He looked over and saw Matt lying there. . . .

He eased the hammer down on the unfired chamber of the ten-gauge and made his way painfully back to the street. There was yet one thing to do. . . .

He picked up his revolver from the dust. He stumbled up the street to the jail, where one horse still was tied. He unwrapped the reins from the rail and swung to the animal's back.

The whole Caine tribe was dead — except for Luke. And Luke was the one he wanted most.

Where would Luke go? Hunted, scared, shocked by the deaths of this brothers . . . Where would he go?

Out on the plain perhaps. But maybe not. Pete's eyes went to the butte.

Luke's horse was just starting up the trail at the head of the street. Then Luke meant to climb to the shelf and explode the dynamite. He meant to have his revenge against the town and the pair who had caused such destruction to his family.

Pete glanced toward the building where he had last seen Jake. Jake was watching Caine but his rifle was not yet up.

Jake would get Luke, if all else failed. He would get him before he could reach the shelf. But Pete wanted Luke alive. He wanted him to stand trial here in Gray Butte and he wanted him to hang.

He dug heels into his horse's sides and pounded up the street. He reached the foot of the trail just as Luke reached its top.

He bawled, "Luke! Caine! Jake's got a rifle on you. If you try to reach the shelf, he'll cut you down just like he did your brothers!"

Caine stared down at him. At this distance it was difficult to make out much of his expression. Pete yelled, "Come on down! You haven't got a chance!"

Still Caine hesitated. Pete's head was reeling. He was growing weaker all the time. If this wasn't over soon . . .

A sudden thought struck him, so simple a thing that he wondered how it had escaped him before. He yelled, "Luke! You can't light that fuse anyway. You haven't got any matches. Remember? You said you were out when we got back to the jail from court this morning."

Luke began to go frantically through his pockets,

191

a difficult task because of his handcuffed wrists. As he finished, his shoulders sagged. He turned his horse and came riding down.

Pete waited until he reached the foot of the trail. Then he reined aside to let Luke pass. He followed Luke down Butte all the way to the jail.

He slid from his horse and followed Caine inside. He locked the cell door behind him, leaving Luke's manacles on.

It was over, he thought. Luke was back in jail, his brothers were dead and their threat to the town removed. The trial could be held and Luke would be convicted of the crime he had confessed.

Pete's head swam crazily. The room tilted and he felt his body strike the floor. A black curtain descended before his eyes. . . .

Chapter 20

The room in which he awoke was strange to him. There were curtains at the windows, a comfortable-looking chair and a thick rug upon the floor.

For several moments he lay still, letting memory bring back all the things that had happened before he passed out in the sheriff's office from loss of blood.

He moved the wounded leg and found it stiff and painful. He peeled back the covers and looked at it, swathed in white bandages on which a hand-sized spot of blood had soaked through and dried.

He pulled himself to a sitting position and stayed there until his head stopped reeling. He reached for the sack of tobacco and papers on the nightstand beside the bed.

He had finished making the cigarette and had lighted it when he heard the door. Doc Bonner stood there looking at him. "Well. So you decided to come around, did you? Put that damned cigarette down!"

Pete grinned at him. "You go to hell. How long

have I been here?"

"This is the second day."

"Who's watching the jail?"

"Jake."

"Caine still there?"

"He's there."

"And the trial. When's it to be?"

"Tomorrow, if you're up to it."

"I'm up to it."

Doc nodded. "I think you are at that. Most of your trouble was that you were just played out."

Pete swung his legs over the side of the bed. "Where's my pants?"

Doc went to the closet. "I got you some clean ones from your room."

He brought them to Pete and Pete put them on. He pulled on his boots and stood up. He stood still until the room stopped whirling. He discovered that he could put his weight on the injured leg without too much difficulty. Shrugging into his shirt he asked, "Town quiet?"

"Same as always. They buried the Caines yesterday afternoon. Jake went up on the butte and lowered the dynamite down."

Pete said, "Julie. Is she . . . ?"

"She's been here three or four times a day."

Pete reached for his holstered gun and belt hanging from the bedpost. He strapped it on. "Think I can make it to the jail?"

"I'll walk with you."

Pete limped painfully down the stairs, with Doc following close behind. He stepped out into the warm morning sunshine. The dizziness was leaving him, though the weakness remained. He hobbled along the street toward Butte, with Doc keeping pace.

People moved along the streets quietly, in sharp contrast to the way things had been before. And something else was different too. Different was the way they looked at Pete. No longer with fear, or hatred, or disapproval. But another way, with respect touched with a bit of awe.

Doc said, "You can get a jury now."

Pete said, "I'm hungry. My God, I could eat a horse!"

"I'll go get you something as soon as we get to the jail."

Pete nodded. "And a gallon of coffee at least."

"All right."

They reached the jail. Pete halted for a moment in front of it and stared up at the butte. People were crazy, he thought, to build a town at the foot of a thing like that. Then he went inside.

Jake was sitting in the sheriff's swivel chair, his feet up on the desk. He got up, grinning.

Pete said, "I didn't get to thank you for the help. I'd have been dead if you hadn't jumped in when you did. You the sheriff now?"

"No. You are. The county commissioners voted to appoint you sheriff to fill out the rest of Stone's term."

Doc said, "I'll get you some breakfast." He turned toward the door but stopped as Julie entered, carrying a tray in her hands. Doc said hastily, "I've got to get back. You ain't the only patient. . . ."

Jake said, "I'll go along too. Now that the sheriff's here, I don't guess there's much for me to do. Be back later, Pete."

Pete nodded, not taking his eyes from Julie's face. He realized that the door leading to the cells was open. He crossed the room and kicked it shut.

Julie's eyes clung to his face as she put the tray down on the desk. She said, "I brought you something to eat. I heard you were up. . . ."

Pete crossed the room to her. He stood for a moment, not touching her, looking down into her eyes.

He saw what he was looking for and opened his arms to her. And suddenly it was as though the nightmare of the past few days had never been. Julie was here, in his arms, where she belonged and where she would always stay.

Lewis B. Patten wrote more than ninety Western novels in thirty years and three of them won Golden Spur Awards from the Western Writers of America and the author himself the Golden Saddleman Award. Indeed, this points up the most remarkable aspect of his work: not that there is so much of it, but that so much of it is excellent. Patten was born in Denver, Colorado, and served in the U.S. Navy 1933–1937. He was educated at the University of Denver during the war years and became an auditor for the Colorado Department of Revenue during the 1940s. It was in this period that he began contributing significantly to Western pulp magazines, fiction that was from the beginning fresh and unique and revealed Patten's lifelong concern with the sociological and psychological effects of group psychology on the frontier. He became a professional writer at the time of his first novel, MASSACRE AT WHITE RIVER (1952). The dominant theme in much of his fiction is the notion of justice, and its opposite, injustice. In his first novel it has to do with exploitation of the Ute Indians, but as he matured as a writer he explored this theme with significant and poignant detail in small towns throughout the early West. Crimes, such as rape or lynching, were often at the center of his stories. When the values embodied in these small towns are examined closely, they are found to be wanting. Conformity is always easier than taking a stand. Yet, in Patten's view of the American West, there is usually a man or a woman who refuses to conform. Among his finest titles, always a difficult choice, would be A KILLING AT KIOWA (1972), RIDE A CROOKED TRAIL (1976), and his many fine contributions to Doubleday's Double D series, including VILLA'S RIFLES (1977) and DEATH RIDES A BLACK HORSE (1978). ⊬

The employees of G.K. HALL hope you have enjoyed this Large Print book. All our Large Print titles are designed for easy reading, and all our books are made to last. Other G.K. Hall Large Print books are available at your library, through selected bookstores, or directly from us. For more information about current and up-coming titles, please call or mail your name and address to:

G.K. HALL
PO Box 159
Thorndike, Maine 04986
800/223-6121
207/948-2962

PN